Dragonbound VI
Green Dragon

Rebecca Shelley

Wonder Realms Books

Cover art © Dusan Kostic | Dreamstime.com
Interior art © Rocich | Dreamstime.com

ISBN-13: 978-0692301937
ISBN-10: 0692301933

Published by Wonder Realms Books

To my son Matthew.

Dragonbound

Prologue

Vasanti tucked the soft purple lichen among the vivid green mosses of her nest and admired the effect the color had on the three iridescent eggs nestled there. Of course, the hatchlings to come would not value her artistic endeavors until they were much older, and by then the nest would be shredded by their little claws and rebuilt many times. That did not stop her from rumbling with contentment as she added delicate orange blossoms around the rim.

Dappled sunlight, filtering through the jungle canopy, shone in through the low entrance and fanned across the expanse of the lair, giving a shimmer of life to her creation. Vasanti licked drops of nectar from the sweet flowers and then licked her eggs, transferring a glossy coat of nectar to add to the eggs' shine.

Outside the lair, tree branches creaked and rustled as her mate made his way back to join her. She watched through the opening as Mahanth leaped from a high branch, spread his front and back legs so the thick skin between them allowed him to glide to the ground. The arched spine on his back helped control his glide, setting him down just outside the lair.

Vasanti. Mahanth crawled into the lair, blocking the sunlight for a moment as his body slid in beside Vasanti's. *I have the most amazing news. You won't believe it.*

News that you were successful hunting and brought back dinner? Vasanti grinned at her mate. Clearly he had forgotten once again that the purpose for his foray away from the lair was to hunt. Or he'd eaten his kill already without bothering to bring some home. Either happened often enough.

Mahanth glanced around as if he had expected food dutifully paralyzed with his poison and clutched in his tail ready to eat. Realizing he'd returned home empty-clawed, he lowered his head, his mottled green skin deepening in shade. *Well . . . no. But there's a reason . . . a good one.*

There's always a reason. No, don't fret. You tend the eggs while I go hunt. We'll eat yet today. Vasanti climbed over top of Mahanth's long tail and slithered out of the lair.

Wait, Vasanti. Mahanth followed her out. *You need to listen to me, because I have something important to tell you.*

Vasanti licked his face. *Whatever is it, dearest?*

2

Mahanth raised his head and looked at her with a spark of unbounded pleasure in his eyes. *I was hunting near the jungle village.*

Vasanti's heart fluttered and she jabbed an admonishing claw into Mahanth's shoulder. *His Majesty, Rajahansa, has warned you not to go near there.*

No. Yes, I mean. He has, but he'll be happy about this.

How so?

I was hunting and I felt something in my mind. One of the human's emotions, a presence, brushing up against my own thoughts. It startled me, but after a moment I tried to talk to this human. She—it was a girl—did not answer me.

Humans cannot hear our speech, Mahanth.

No, but the Nagas can. And it occurred to me that His Majesty has waited a long, long time for a female Naga to be born in the village. Don't you see? This is wonderful, Vasanti. If I catch this girl and bring her to Rajahansa, he will reward us. We'll never have to hunt for our own food again. He'll let us live in the palace and feed with the gold dragons. You'll have gold and jewels to line your nest with instead of moss.

Jewels aren't very soft. The hatchlings will need a soft nest until their scales harden up. Vasanti rested a restraining foreclaw on Mahanth's shoulder. *Even if this girl is a Naga, Rajahansa will find her without your help. The villagers will call him as soon as she comes down with the dragon fever.* Vasanti was used to Mahanth's crazy schemes, but this one made her shiver. Too much could go wrong in dealing with the villagers, and Rajahansa *had* forbidden them to go anywhere near the humans.

What if they don't? What if something happens to her before then? She's often in the jungle, too far from the village to be safe. She goes off alone—the fountain knows why the older humans let her. Mahanth shook Vasanti's claw off him. *We can't risk her life so carelessly, and I refuse to give up the reward that is rightfully mine for finding her.* Mahanth slithered off into the jungle. The thick ferns on the ground pushed aside as he moved through them and then sprang back, hiding his passage as if he'd never been there.

Mahanth, wait, Vasanti called. *Come back. Don't do this.* When Mahanth did not respond, Vasanti crawled after him a few feet, stopped, and turned back to the lair. The eggs. She couldn't leave the eggs unguarded. She returned to the lair and tried calling Mahanth back again.

He ignored her.

She paced back and forth in front of the lair, desperate to go after him, sure he had run off into trouble over his head. But the eggs. She had to guard the eggs.

Mahanth. Mahanth, she pleaded.

Quiet now, he said. *I'm in no danger. It is only one unarmed human girl, and she has strayed far from the village.*

Leave her alone. Just leave her alone. Come back now, Mahanth. Vasanti shuddered. When he got things stuck in his head like this, he never would listen to reason. Her agitation turned to motion. She jumped up and clawed at the ground above the lair, rocks dirt, moss, leaves all fell down beneath her, covering the hole. Then she streaked off into the jungle after her opportunistic mate.

She found his body sometime later, crumpled to the ground, dead, with a crossbow bolt through his chest. A single bolt straight to the heart. A ways off, a group of villagers carried a feverish young man in mismatched armor toward their home. He had the death weapon, a crude crossbow, strapped to his back. Not long afterward, while Vasanti still lay curled beside Mahanth's stiff body, she heard the great gong sound, calling the Naga king to the village to retrieve the new Naga.

When Vasanti had cried herself out, she left her dead mate and returned to the lair, clawing the entrance open so she could rejoin her unhatched children.

Chapter One

Tana carried the breakfast tray into the king's chambers. Unlike so many of the other Nagas, his room was his own, separate from his dragon's. It was big enough that four of the village huts could easily fit inside it. Tana stepped on the plush red rug that covered the floor. It made her nervous walking on something so moss-like. Mani, the queen, sat on the bed that's frame was shaped like a silver serpent leaping from ocean waves. Her vacant eyes stared at the picture of herself on the wall across from her, but she saw nothing. Liander sat next to her, a sharp jungle knife clutched in his hand. That meant Rajahansa was still sleeping.

"Good morning, Your Majesties." Tana set the tray on the table next to the bed.

Liander leaned over and grabbed a sweet cake off the tray. "It's about time. I'm starving."

His Majesty, King Amar, stirred in his spot by the wall. Chains clanked as he rose to his feet. Chains with no lock or key. The shackles had been fused around Amar's wrists with Naga power and secured the same way to the palace wall. The chains held him away from his wife with barely enough room to stand or sit.

While Rajahansa was awake, the dragon's mind blocked Amar from using his own power to free himself from the chains. While Rajahansa slept, Liander's knife, hovering over Mani, kept him equally bound.

"Good Morning, Tana. Are you well?" Amar's golden robe was wrinkled and stained. His face gaunt from the daily mental battles he fought with his dragon.

"I am well, thank you." Tana's eyes stung.

Amar frowned as she took him his plate of fruit and sweet cakes. "From the bleak look in your eyes, I see that you are still unhappy here at the palace."

"How can I be happy with you chained like this?" She turned a glare on Liander.

Liander stood, fingering the knife. His gaze was cold on her. "Silence, Girl. You bring the food. You keep your mouth shut. Or I'll shut it for you."

Heat rose to Tana's face. "You aren't man enough to even touch me."

"No?" Liander grabbed her, dragged her up against his chest, and forced his lips down onto her own.

The stale scent of his sweat, mixed with the taste of sweet cake on his mouth, made her gag. She struggled in his grasp, but the cold edge of the hunting knife against the back of her neck stilled her.

"Liander, stop!" Amar shouted. The chains rattled and went silent.

Liander left off kissing her and swung her around so he could press the blade hard against her throat. The king had manipulated the metal of one of the shackles, freeing his right hand.

"Put the shackle back on," Liander said, "or I'll kill her."

"You won't kill her. You need her." Amar got his other arm free.

"But we don't need your wife."

Both men stood unmoving, gauging the distance between each of them and Mani, wondering which of them could reach her first. Mani gave no notice of either man. Haidar had stripped her mind of free will, leaving her nothing more than a shell. She could not even feed herself. Tana had to do it.

Liander shoved Tana aside and dove toward Mani. Amar lunged, tackling Liander just before his knife would have struck her. The two men hit the floor, wrestling for the knife.

A roar from Rajahansa rattled the bookshelves. The Great Gold dragon appeared at the window, coming into view as he left behind the sunlight, landed on the sill, and forced his neck, chest, and forearms inside the room. He flicked Liander aside, grabbed Amar, lifted him into the air and shook him. His gold dragonstone flashed as dragon and Naga battled with each other mind-to-mind.

Liander climbed to his feet and went over to Mani, pressing the tip of the knife against her tender flesh.

Rajahansa dropped Amar next to the wall where his chains waited.

"Put the chains back on," Liander ordered.

Amar rubbed his head. His chest heaved as if he'd fought a battle against a dozen men. "All right," he said when he'd drawn enough air into his lungs to speak. "I'll do it. Don't hurt her. Just . . . by the fountain, leave the women alone. They should be treated with respect and care. Whatever is wrong between us, don't take it out on the women."

Rajahansa slapped the shackles back on Amar's arms and manipulated the metal to lock them there. Then he withdrew from the window and flapped away.

Amar slumped to the ground and put his head in his hands, exhausted beyond any more use of his power.

"Get out," Liander ordered Tana.

Tana took a step backwards toward the door. "But I haven't fed Mani yet."

Liander's face twisted into a cruel smile. "Don't worry. I can make her eat." He touched the side of her forehead, and Mani's arm jerked up and reached for the tray of food.

Amar choked back a quiet sob.

Tana turned and ran from the room. She rushed down the hall, passing tapestries and paintings of dragons and men, arched doorways and chambers hung with jeweled chandeliers, alcoves with statues of dragons and their Nagas. She would trade all the wealth and grandeur of the castle for one more day at home in her little wooden hut. One more day of freedom.

This was Kanvar's fault. He'd promised not to tell anyone about her connections with the dragons and a moment later broken his promise. For her own welfare, of course, because she'd die if she didn't bond with a dragon, and he'd been sure she'd be safe and happy at the palace, confident in the kind nature of his father and brother. Such a sweet family, and no man more gentle than Amar, and no one more gallant and polite as Devaj.

Tana half-smiled at the thought of Devaj, certainly no other man was as handsome as him. And Kanvar, her betrayer, her savior from both Great Green and red volcanic dragon, her friend. Maybe more. The last time they'd seen each other he had held her, kissed her forehead. Devaj was all cool gold, gentle and thoughtful, while Kanvar was fire and anger and passion. Her heart was torn between the two brothers, not that Devaj had made any move to claim her. But now they were both gone and the king chained, the palace had become a prison. Hadn't Kanvar called it that? Yes, and she'd told him it was beautiful. And it was, for a short while, before everything came crashing down.

Tana had almost reached her own chambers when Haidar's voice cut through the hall. "You're up early."

His voice gave her cold chills. "I had to feed the queen since you destroyed her mind."

"Oh, Tana. I didn't destroy it. I just tucked it away for a while. We can't have her causing trouble." Haidar put a reassuring hand on Tana's shoulder.

She'd sooner be touched by a mud toad. "Leave me alone." She shrugged his hand off, but he grabbed her arm instead.

"Don't pull away from me. You know I love you."

"You don't know what love is."

"Yes, I do." He caressed her cheek with his other hand. "It's what you and I will have as we replenish the pure Naga race."

Tana didn't try to pull away again. He could hold her with his hand or with his mind, either way she had no escape from Haidar. She rubbed her hand across her bruised lips. "Liander might object to that. He seems to have claimed me for himself."

"Nonsense. I'm the older brother. You are mine by right."

"What right? This has nothing to do with your rights. My right is to choose whatever man I wish to marry, or none at all if I want to remain single. You cannot force me to accept you as husband."

"Can't I? And who's going to stop me? Amar is power-less. My father is a weak old fool. Liander wouldn't dare cross me. I had an older brother once who might have, but he is dead, killed by the humans he tried to befriend."

"Kanvar will stop you."

Haidar snorted. "Kanvar is a walking dead man. His dragon will not survive much longer without Parmver's medicine. He can't fly, which means he can't hunt, which means he can't eat. He's doomed to a slow death by starvation if the other blue dragons don't find him first and give him the swifter option."

Tana shuddered. Kanvar had not mentioned anything to her about his dragon not being able to fly.

"Oh, don't worry." Haidar ran his hand down the full length of her braid, his fingers brushing down her back to her waist and his hand resting there. "I'll be very gentle with you. And you will love me. I promise." His mind, like his hand, caressed her thoughts, igniting a longing in her. "See, you will enjoy your life with me."

He pulled away from her, leaving her flushed and out of breath, thoughts of Kanvar flown from her mind.

Haidar pressed a hand against her forehead. "Well, you don't feel hot yet. But don't worry, I'm sure the fever will be upon you soon. You have been spending plenty of time with the dragons Rajahansa has chosen for you to pick from. The touch of the gold dragons will speed your need to bond. And on the day that you bond, we will marry."

He kissed her cheek. "Good day, my love."

Footsteps echoed down the golden hall as he walked away. Choking back tears, Tana hurried into her chambers and locked the door behind her. Not that the lock would stop anyone in the palace besides Aadi.

"I hate him," Tana mumbled under her breath as she slumped on the bed and picked up her sewing. "I hate them both. Not sure which I hate more." Liander with his brutality or Haidar with his subtle cruelty. How could the sons of such a sweet old man be so rotten?

Her hands shook, making it hard for her to thread the needle. A few more stitches and she'd be finished with the robe she would wear for her Bonding Ceremony. She'd already suffered through three Choosing Ceremonies, being forced to look into the minds and hearts of gold dragons who were loyal to Rajahansa. He only allowed her around those who shared his thirst for the restoration of Stonefountain and the Nagas return to power over the human world. She could not be sure if he had twisted their minds to this thinking or if they had come by the desires naturally. But it sickened her what they were willing to do, what they were already planning in their minds and hearts to regain domination for the Great Gold dragons. She had chosen none of them, and Rajahansa had grown angrier and angrier with her.

She got the needle threaded and paused to scratch the itch on her chest, which had grown more persistent each passing day. Parmver's ointment had helped stop the spread of the rash so far, but she didn't know for how long. Not long enough. This robe would have to be finished today.

Shivering with a sudden chill, she set to work and did not stop until Aadi came to her door. She could tell his knock from the others. His was more of a question instead of a demand.

"Just a moment." She slid the last wooden dowel, stolen from various tapestries in her room and around the palace, into place and sewed it in.

Aadi knocked again. "Tana, open up. It's time for our training with Parmver."

"All right. I'm coming." Tana set the robe aside and returned the needle to the pincushion. The garment was ready. She could only hope it would work the way she intended it to.

Kanvar squinted to see as the morning fog started to dissipate. Conserving energy, Dharanidhar glided along the western coast of Kundiland, letting the sea breeze keep him aloft. The gray ocean waves tossed against rocky outcroppings, sending up sprays of white. Thick trees blanketed the mainland, growing to the very edge of the beaches and headlands, sending twisted branches out over rocky cliffs pummeled by water.

It's no use, Dharanidhar grumbled to Kanvar. *The ocean along the west coast is too angry.*

Kanvar rubbed his hand along Dhar's cool mist-slicked neck where he sat harnessed to Dharanidhar's back. *Perhaps one of the others has found something.*

I doubt it. This search is hopeless. Dharanidhar's wing ached. Searching for a new nesting ground would be better accomplished by younger dragons, but younger dragons would not have the wisdom to know the features to look for, and all who could fight were needed elsewhere. *We'll never find the right place*, Dharanidhar complained.

Well, if the right place were easy to find, it wouldn't be the right place, would it? Kanvar felt bad that it was his fault the gold dragons had found the Great Blue dragons' nesting ground in the high mountains.

For so many years the Great Blue dragon pride had been safe there. No longer. Once again the Great Blue dragons were being forced to flee their home and find another.

They could not return to the east coast with the human war fleets soon to land there. They would not fly to the other side of the world where the Naga lords still ruled. Their blood called them to the ocean, which was their natural place, flying free, their blue scales blending with water and sky. The salty moisture. The cool wind. Fish and seals to dive and swim and hunt. The oldest dragons of the pride had spent long now searching, searching, flying along the coast, bickering over this place and that. One place was too exposed, another to small, most too battered by the waves for safe nesting.

Dharanidhar and Kanvar had flown south while others searched to the north. Dharanidhar had barely recovered from the scourging at the hands of Rajahansa and the gold dragons before setting out in search of new nesting grounds. Kanvar used the term *recovered* loosely. Dhar would never recover, but he had accepted the pain now as a necessary part of his life. Dharanidhar's aches made Kanvar restless, but that was not the only reason he was anxious to find a place for the Great Blue dragon pride. Time was scarce before the human armies arrived, and he didn't know how long Anilon's best fighters could keep Rajahansa pinned at the golden palace, unable to drag Amar to Stonefountain and release Khalid.

There's a nice place, Kanvar said, resting his gaze on a sheltered bay with white sandy beaches. A carpet of emerald trees swept almost down to the sand. Dharanidhar wheeled and flew toward it.

Kanvar! Devaj's bright voice in his mind startled him.

Elkatran, Devaj's dragon appeared out of the mist, clutching a net which contained a wooden platform loaded with villagers and supplies. He let it down beside the trees and settled onto the sand. Bensharie followed, carrying a man on his back and a wooden trunk in each claw.

Snorting, Dharanidhar landed beside the two gold dragons and folded his aching wings up against his sides. Devaj waved at Kanvar from Elkatran's back. "What brings you here, Kanvar?" he called.

"We were—" A glance at the tree line showed a number of villagers already settling into the spot and building huts. "So this is the safe place you're moving the jungle village to?" It seemed the best place Dharanidhar and Kanvar had seen yet was already claimed by the humans.

Yes, do you like it? Bensharie said. He fluttered his wings, pleased with the work he and Elkatran were doing.

"I like it a lot," Kanvar said.

Dharanidhar let out an angry growl.

A worried frown crossed Devaj's face. "Your joints are swollen again, Dhar," he said. "Are those new scars? It looks like someone has shredded your wings. We've been so worried about you since you went to free Father from

Rajahansa and never came back. What happened?"

Dharanidhar growled again. Angry. Feral. Mortified by his defeat at the hands of the gold dragon. He bared his teeth and stoked his fires.

Kanvar tensed. "We tried to free Father. We failed. Rajahansa plans to take him to Stonefountain and give him to Khalid to possess. Khalid has promised him a way to defeat the human armies in exchange. But the Great Blue dragons are guarding the east coast, making sure Rajahansa can't get to Stonefountain. Dhar and I have been looking for . . . you. It seems we've found you. He needs medicine, Devaj. He needs it now. Will you make it for him?" Kanvar rubbed Dharanidhar's neck, trying to sooth his friend.

"I have some ready," Devaj said, sliding off of Elk-atran's neck. "I was frightened they'd killed you though, when we heard nothing at all. I've been searching for you with my mind but couldn't feel you."

"We've been shielded." Kanvar unbuckled the harness that held him to Dharanidhar's back. "Couldn't risk the gold dragons finding us."

Dharanidhar growled again and blue fire crackled between his teeth.

"How's Devaj to get medicine for you if you roast him alive?" Kanvar said. Dharanidhar's pride was hurt. He'd lost a battle and lived, run away, been hiding in fear of another attack. The shame of it hurt more than his battered body. Yet he lived, for Kanvar's sake, and because the Great Blue dragon pride needed him to find them a safe place for the women and children—a lowly task for a crippled old dragon.

As soon as Kanvar's feet hit the sand, Dharanidhar turned his back and lumbered away to sulk on the beach. No, he wouldn't fight Elkatran and Devaj, no matter how mortified he was. They needed all the allies they could get.

What's wrong with him? Bensharie asked, troubled.

"He's hurt," Kanvar said, "and he's in a very bad mood. I wouldn't suggest trying to talk to him. He'd probably eat your for breakfast."

Bensharie shuddered and went to help the villagers.

Chapter Two

Ignoring Aadi sitting on Parmver's bed reading as if it came as easily to him as breathing, Tana forced her mouth to make the sound of each letter on the page that Parmver pointed to. Her forehead tensed with frustration.

"That's very good," Parmver said. He shifted his old body in the chair at the desk beside her. "You'll be reading in no time."

"No time. That's exactly what I have. I need to understand what these books say now."

Parmver patted her shoulder, and using his cane, dragged himself to his feet. Ceiron, his dragon, snorted in pain. His vast body lay curled up, taking up much of the room, his skin stretched brittle across his bones, his eyes watery. The chamber smelled of ancient flesh and decaying teeth.

Parmver lost his balance and tipped, but Tana jumped to her feet and steadied him. "Are you all right?"

Parmver shook his head. "My herbs have run out. There is nothing you can do."

Panic caught Tana's breath, and she pressed her hand against her chest. "All of them?"

Parmver nodded. "Just the ones I've been using a lot."

"Can't you get more?" It's over, Tana thought. It's over today. She'd had chills for the last hour. If Parmver didn't serve her his "herbal tea" with their lesson, nothing would keep her fever at bay and hidden from Haidar.

"No, I can't get more," Parmver said. His hands shook on the head of his cane. His body shook. Ceiron moaned. "You know Rajahansa sealed the passage down to the jungle through my lab. Even if I could manipulate a hole in the stone without him noticing, I'm too old to make it down the steps to the jungle, and he's now forbidden the young dragons to gather the herbs for me."

"He's trying to kill you? He knows you need those herbs for your medicine." Tana couldn't believe it.

"Of course His Majesty isn't trying to kill Parmver," Aadi said. "He just can't risk letting the young dragons out while we're at war with the Great Blue dragons. They think Great Gold dragon flesh is a delicacy and fight over who will eat the heart."

"They do not," Parmver snapped. "Who's telling you such lies?"

Aadi lifted his chin in defiance. "Haidar said he saw them do it."

Parmver let out a long, slow breath before speaking again. "Aadi, just go back to your studies."

Aadi yawned then planted his face in the open book he'd been reading. "Please, Parmver, can lessons be done for today? I've read this book ten times. Believe me, I get the idea. King Khalid was a tyrant. He used his powers for evil. We should never, never mess with people's minds or force them to do something they don't want to." Aadi's head snapped up. "I know. Why don't you let me read that book you have about how to manipulate things?"

Parmver hobbled to the bookshelf that lined the walls of the chamber and pressed a gnarled and shaking hand against a locked bookcase. "No, Aadi. Not yet. You haven't even bonded. Manipulating takes more concentration and control than you can imagine. Perhaps in a few decades you will advance to these other books."

"What about summoning?" Aadi jumped to his feet and let his book drop to the floor. "Then if I lose one of my shoes again, I could just call it to me. You wouldn't have to chide me to remember where I put things."

"No." Parmver's voice turned sharp. "Aadi, if you don't care to learn what I wish to teach you today then go find something else to do. Be gone. Get out. We'll pick up where we left off tomorrow."

"Fine." Aadi kicked the book aside and darted from the room.

Parmver made it the few steps back to his chair and collapsed into it. "I'm sorry, Tana," he said in a wavering voice. "I would give you more tea if I could, but we've used the last of it. Time is running out for both of us, I think. And now I find out Haidar is poisoning Aadi's mind with lies. Oh, Tana. What are we going to do?"

Tana sat down beside Parmver and took his trembling hand. "Why is Haidar so cruel? Why is he doing these things?"

Parmver let out a soft, despairing laugh. "This palace, hanging on the face of a cliff thousands of feet above the tallest tree, how do you suppose it got here?"

Tana shook her head. "I never thought about it."

"How did you build your hut in the village?"

"I had to cut the sticks from trees, clear them of leaves and twigs, haul them up onto the platform, then put them together."

"How did you make the platform?"

"That's much harder. The planks have to be cut and smoothed just right. Then, they have to be hoisted into the tree and secured in place."

"How did you hoist them?"

"With a rope and pulley. We hang the pulley high up in the tree and loop the rope through. Then, we can haul things up and down."

"How would you hang a pulley in the sky to hoist the bricks of the palace up here?"

Tana rubbed her head. The fever she had held at bay for so long came on her hard now that she'd missed her dose of Parmver's medicine. His talk of palace construction confused her and made her head hurt. "I don't know."

"You can't. There is no pulley big enough, no ropes long enough, no trees tall enough to build this palace where it is. And yet Haidar and Liander built it. They and their dragons cut and shaped every stone from the quarry. The dragons carried each stone up here and held it while my boys manipulated the rock to lock it in place. It took them a hundred years to build this palace. Every inch of it created with their own sweat and blood. And Kanvar in his stubborn-headed rebellion has compromised that. All their work, a lifetime of building and refining, imperiled by Kanvar's actions. If you had worked so long and hard on your home, would you abandon it to hide or would you defend it? I'm not saying the way Haidar and Liander are behaving is right. It's not, but they have just cause for their anger and desire to fight the humans. They had an older brother, did you know? My first born son was betrayed and murdered by a human he thought was his friend. Their sister and Amar's father were killed by dragon hunters. Haidar and Liander have much reason to hate."

Tana shivered. Parmver's chamber had grown too cold, or she had grown too hot. "What can we do? There must be something."

"You . . . can go back to your studies." Shaking, Parmver retrieved a book from the bookshelf and handed it to her. "I know you can't read yet, but this has pictures. It teaches the most basic concepts about being a Naga. Many of which we have already discussed, you and I. How to shield your mind for privacy, how to interact telepathically with your dragon."

Tana opened the book and turned the brittle pages, taking in the pictures that depicted a Choosing Ceremony and a Bonding Ceremony and beyond.

"The book is divided into three sections," Parmver said. "Naga powers fall into three categories—communicating, manipulating, and summoning. The things I have been teaching you all fall under communicating. That is hard enough to master at first. Your power, the power of your mind when you bond with your dragon, has the potential to be used for much good or much evil. Control is not easy to master, and you could hurt someone without even meaning to. Kanvar and Aadi are both anxious to learn more, but neither are ready."

Tana stopped turning the pages at a picture that showed a young Naga standing beside a canvas with a half finished painting. One hand held a brush, the other was pressed against the canvas with the unfinished picture taking shape beneath his palm. "What's this?"

"Manipulating. One of the more genteel and pleasant uses of the power. The artist applies the colors to the canvas with the brush, then uses his power to shape them into the exact image he has in his mind. The trick is, of course, you have to have a very clear image in your thoughts or the painting comes out looking like mud." Parmver laughed, a genuine laugh of pleasure. "You see, Tana, it's all about control and clear thinking. Controlling one's own mind is the hardest skill any man or woman will have to master."

"Yes, sir." Tana turned a few more pages and came to a picture of a boy with his hand outstretched, palm upward. Floating in the air above his hand was a small golden ball. "What's this?"

Parmver cleared his throat. "Levitation. Another form of manipulation. A difficult one. Took me forever to master."

"You can do this?" Tana looked up from the book at the old man.

Parmver smiled and shook his head. "It's a needless waste of energy, used by vain Nagas to show off. It takes much concentration and control. I have no need to show off at my age."

"Can you levitate yourself?" Tana walked past Ceiron to the window and stared down the cliffs to the jungle canopy far below.

Parmver gave her a wan smile. "At my best, I managed a foot off the ground once."

"What if you fell? Could you use it to stop yourself from falling?"

"Tana." Parmver took her hand and eased her away from the window. "In my youth, my friends and I spent a good long time exploring that notion. I broke my leg twice, my hand, my collar bone, and my arm, jumping off the roof of our family mansion."

"Right." Tana went back to turning pages. "That won't help us. We need something else."

"What exactly are you looking for?" Parmver hobbled to the bed and sat down, nestling his cane between his knees. "You can't escape this palace, and even if you could, you would die. You have to bond with a gold dragon, Tana. I know you don't like the ones you've met so far, but you will find one that is right for you. I'm sure of it."

"How will I know what dragon is right?"

"You will see the dragon in your mind. You will feel her in your heart. The two of you will be pulled toward each other like magnets."

"Magnets?"

Parmver waved a hand. "Never mind that. We don't have time for a science lesson. You will be attracted to your dragon like a hummingbird to sweet nectar. Have you ever in your life felt some dragon present in your mind, like . . .

like she is a part of you that you have just forgotten or not yet discovered?"

Tana took a deep breath and closed her eyes. Her thoughts went immediately to her safe place, a place she had imagined for herself long ago. A burrow dug out from the ground beneath a hill, with a narrow entrance, but wide and open inside. Moss and lichen grew on the walls, not just randomly, but with their colors blending to form pictures as vibrant as the best tapestries in the palace. In the center of the burrow was a nest, soft and inviting, safe. Something . . . someone crooned over her and rubbed a scaly hand down her back as if soothing a child. That someone had always been in this place, ever since the day Tana had first imagined it. The day her mother died. Tana looked up from the nest into the gentle eyes of a Great Green dragon.

"Tana, no." Parmver's hand squeezed hers, pulling her away from the burrow. "You can't bond with a Great Green dragon. This can't be. It will never work." Parmver's hand on hers shook with agitation. "You can't ride a green dragon. They do not fly. The frill on their backs would get in the way. Worse, the poison. Tana, you'd never even be able to touch this dragon without being paralyzed. You must, Must, block this daydream from your mind. Think of the gold dragons. Sense those around you here. Haidar has not turned all of them to hate. You must find a dragon you are physically and mentally compatible with."

Tana pulled away from Parmver, anger bubbling up inside her. Who was he to tell her what type of dragon she should bond with? "Kanvar bonded with a Great Blue dragon and was not hurt by it. Karishi's dragon is a metal dragon, for goodness sake. You asked me what dragon I was attracted to, and I have shown you. You can't think worse of me for it."

"Tana. I don't think worse of you. I just fear for your life."

"It's not my life you should fear for, but your own . . . and the king's." Tana turned her attention back to the book. Parmver was distracting her from her purpose.

"What is this?" She turned the book so Parmver could see two pictures side by side on the page. In the first, a Naga held out his hand toward the same golden ball that had been levitating. Now it sat on a shelf across the room from the Naga. In the next picture, the Naga held the ball in his hand.

"Summoning." Parmver's voice was low. "The hardest skill to master. Aadi was out of his mind to think I could teach him anything about that at this point in his life."

"What is summoning?"

"Like the picture shows, the ability to call some object directly to you from some other place."

"You make it float to you, like levitating?"

"No. It disappears from where it is and reappears in your hand."

"Through walls?"

"Through anything. Well, not really *through* anything. It simply ceases to exist where it is and re-exists in your hand. Tana, you can't even begin to imagine the level of power and control this takes. You have to be so familiar with the object that it literally becomes a part of you for a moment. It's not a game or a toy. It's dangerous. You could hurt yourself, kill yourself, if you try to do this before you're ready."

Tana glanced down at the picture. "Clearly, this is not something I can learn. But you . . . can you summon things?"

Parmver cleared his throat. "I have mastered that ability. There are some small items I have become familiar with enough to summon."

"Can you summon the chains off the king?"

Parmver rose to his feet, shaking. "What? No. I have no knowledge of these chains, no affinity with them, and they have been manipulated to be part of the wall itself. I'd have to summon the whole wall. That's crazy talk."

"What about the king, could you summon him here? And the queen?" Tana's heartbeat vibrated her chest. Perhaps this was it, finally a way to free Amar and Mani.

Parmver shook his head. His scratchy voice rose, "No. No, no. You can't summon or manipulate living things."

"I know, I can't, but you—"

"No, I can't. No one can. Living things cannot be summoned."

"How do you know? You could try. At least you could try. You've known Amar his whole life. You can feel his mind. If you had any connection with anything more than your own dragon it would be him. Please, Parmver, we have to save him."

"Living things can *not* be summoned." Parmver tapped his cane against the ground, accenting each word.

"But, Parmver."

"No. Look, I'll show you." Parmver held out his hand and a violet orchid appeared in his palm, but the moment it appeared, the flower petals turned black and crumbled to dust. "Something about the nature of manipulating or summoning destroys living organisms. Believe me, Tana, I've been churning my mind for days, trying to think of any way to use my powers that could free him. I haven't found any answers."

Tana slammed the book closed and thumped it down on the desk. "Clarity of thought, clarity and control. That's what we need, like you said. The most important things. But neither of us can think straight. You're in too much pain, and I've got this blasted fever burning through my mind."

"Clarity," Parmver mumbled, echoing her words. "We need clarity. Or . . ." He jumped to his feet, almost stumbling over his cane as he rushed to a wardrobe on the far side of his bed. He pulled open the doors and started tearing clothes from the hangers, throwing them in a pile behind him, followed by shoes and other oddments. He must have cleared the whole wardrobe out to get to a small chest at the bottom that looked like it hadn't seen the light of day in hundreds of years. The metal clasp on the chest was sealed shut, but Parmver manipulated it open.

Tana held her breath as he reached inside and pulled out a tiny iron box. "We don't need clarity and control, Tana. We need just the opposite. And your thought of summoning has given me a brilliant idea. He hobbled back to the desk and set the box down. "Don't touch it. Don't open it. Not yet."

Grinning, he held both his gnarled hands out in front of him palms up. A sheathed sword appeared in them. The handle was inlaid with gold.

Tana gasped. "What's that?"

"The king's sword. It is powerful, quenched in the waters of Stonefountain when it was forged. Don't touch the hilt. It will shock anyone not of the royal line. This sword can cut through anything. And this—" Parmver tapped the little iron box, "—came into my hands on the night Stonefountain fell. I traded my only dose of elixir for the coughing sickness to get it. It is our best chance to free the king."

Chapter Three

Shivering and dizzy from the dragon fever, Tana carried the lunch tray into the king's chambers. Liander, who had been sleeping on the bed while Rajahansa was awake for the day, sat up and rubbed his eyes. He grinned at Tana.

"Tana, dearest. My day would be so boring without you. I hope you brought better food for lunch than you did for breakfast."

"I bring what I'm given by the young dragons who prepare it." She set the tray on the desk and picked up the bowl of creamed mushroom soup to feed Mani.

Liander snatched the bottle of the palace's best vintage wine from the tray.

"Hey, that's for the king." Tana grabbed it back from him. "I brought the water for you. Haidar doesn't want you drunk on the job."

Liander grabbed her wrist and exerted a crushing grip until the bottle loosed from her hand. "Take something from me again and I'll beat you."

"Liander, I warned you not to harm the women," Amar called from his place by the wall.

"Shut up, Majesty. Tana's the one who started this fight. Everything she gets, she asked for." Liander pulled the cork from the bottle, grabbed an empty goblet from the tray, and poured himself a drink. He emptied the goblet and filled it again before taking his plate with the roasted bovinder pie.

In the mean time, Tana pressed spoonfuls of the soup into the queen's mouth and made sure she swallowed them. Sweat trickled into Tana's eyes, but she shivered with cold chills.

Liander made it halfway through his pie before he yawned and slumped back on the bed beside his wicked jungle knife. The goblet fell from his slack grasp and hit the plush red carpet, spilling the last drops of its contents.

"What?" King Amar jumped to his feet with surprise and alarm on his face.

Tana pressed a finger to her lips and set the bowl of soup down on the bedside table. As she carried the king's lunch to him, her movement felt restrained and awkward. The dress she wore was loose enough, it was what was strapped to her waist beneath the billowing folds of cloth that threatened to trip her. Despite that, she'd made it to the kitchen and then to the king's chamber without anyone noticing something amiss.

"Here you go, Your Majesty." She set the plate on the floor beside him. The scent of the roasted bovinder mixed with the savory smell of the perfectly-golden pie crust. One thing she could say about the palace, the food here was good. "Eat, Please." She motioned to the meal.

The king glanced to Liander, unconscious on the bed, and then back to Tana. "What have you done?"

Her face flushed. She was hoping to do what she had to do while the king was focusing on his food not looking at her. "Nothing yet, Majesty. How is Rajahansa?"

Amar scowled. "He's busy arguing with Parmver. He should not say the things he's saying. I fear Rajahansa will hurt him."

Tana nodded. Good, their plan was working; Parmver had Rajahansa distracted. Taking a deep breath, she loosed the ties on her dress and pulled it off over her head.

Amar gasped and turned away. His face went scarlet.

"What?" Tana said, her fingers shaking as she unclasped the sword belt at her waist. "You've never seen a woman in petticoats before?"

"Tana, Please." The king's voice was tight.

Parmver had wrapped the sword hilt in fabric, but Tana did her best to touch only the sheath anyway as she pulled the sword and belt away from her body and held it out to the king.

With his face averted, Amar did not see what she held out to him.

"Your Majesty." Tana grabbed his hand and pressed the sword into it. Then she turned from him and put her dress back on. When she faced him again, he held the sword still sheathed in his hands, looking between it and Mani.

"I can't. They'll kill her."

"No. You will run, and take her with you."

The king's hands tightened on the sheath so hard his knuckles turned white. "Run where? I could not carry her far or fast."

Tana pulled from her pocket a little leather pouch that was hung on a golden cord and hurried over to Mani. She put the cord around Mani's neck so the pouch waited empty on her chest. "Parmver says the sword can cut through rock. You must run down to his lab and cut through to the stairs in the cliff that leads down into the jungle. Be swift, you must get below the jungle canopy before Rajahansa catches you."

Amar shook his head. "Mani can't run."

"Yes, she can." Tana fingered the little iron box in her pocket. "Cut the chains now, quickly and grab whatever you think you'll need to survive in the jungle. Parmver says you have things always packed to go at any time. In a moment, Rajahansa will be alerted to trouble."

King Amar drew the sword but hesitated. "This can't work. Rajahansa is blocking my power. I can't free Mani's mind."

"You won't have to." Tana pulled out the little iron box and held it up for Amar to see. "Sorry, Your Majesty. Parmver tells me this is going to hurt." She opened the lid and pulled out the stone. A searing scream of music cut through her mind. Already weakened from the fever, the pain of the singing stone was too much for Tana. The iron box and the stone fell from her fingers and hit the floor. The blue glow of the stone looked sickly against the red carpet. Tana told herself to pick it up, but she couldn't move, couldn't breathe. Her eyes watered. Nothing Parmver had said had prepared her for this.

Chains clanked behind her. The king's hand steadied her as he scoped up the singing stone with his other hand and slid it into the pouch on Mani's neck.

Mani blinked and looked around as if coming out of a deep sleep. "Amar, what's happening?" She grabbed the pouch at her neck.

"Leave it. We must move quickly." Amar kissed her cheek, grabbed the iron box from the floor, and tucked it into his pocket. Then he threw open a chest at the foot of his bed and grabbed a bundle from within—green dragon-scale armor, a crossbow, and other dragon hunter supplies, cleaned, packed, and waiting for use.

He grabbed Mani's arm and raced for the door, and still Tana stood frozen in place, terrified by the song and the stone that shivered her to the very center of her bones.

Amar got the door open and turned back. "Tana. You must come with us."

She nodded but couldn't move.

"Tana." The king came back for her, grabbed her hand, and drew her toward the door.

The movement jarred her enough she remembered what she was about. "Wait." She pulled away from Amar long enough to grab Liander's jungle knife and tuck it away between her dress and petticoat. Then she rushed with the king and the queen out of the room and through the palace, working their way inward toward the door that led down into the cliff face itself, down to Parmver's lab and beyond.

Just as they reached the door, Haidar's frantic voice rang through the halls. "Rajahansa, there's a stone." His footsteps clattered toward them.

Amar and Mani dashed through the door, but instead of following them, Tana closed the door behind them and ran in the direction of Haidar's voice. She had to distract him, stop him from following the sound of the singing stone, buy the king and queen time to get away.

"Haidar," Tana cried out as soon as he came in sight. "What is it? It hurts so much." She grabbed his arm, hanging on him, looking at him to protect her.

"The greatest evil ever loosed in the world, a singing stone," Haidar said. He clenched his teeth and wrapped a protective arm around her. "I don't know how our enemies could have gotten one into the castle. I've posted guards everywhere. Hurry. We must find this intruder and stop him. It sounded like he went this way."

Haidar hurried Tana with him toward the door down to Parmver's lab.

"Haidar." Tana filled her voice with alarm and clutched Haidar even tighter. "What if the stone is a distraction to pull all the guards away from His Majasty, Rajahansa. The blue dragons, they could kill him."

Haidar hesitated, torn between going after whoever carried the singing stone and running to protect Rajahansa. His loyalty to the king won out. Dragging Tana with him, he ran to a giant golden throne room, one of the few halls in the palace without windows. Parmver had chosen this spot purposely for his confrontation with Rajahansa.

"There's a singing stone," Haidar cried, rushing into the room. "We must prepare for attack. It has to be the blue dragons."

Rajahansa roared and his dragonstone flashed. He had Parmver in his hand, the sharp claw of his thumb pressing against Parmver's chest.

"I can't understand you," Haidar said. "The stone, I can still hear it, but it's moving away."

Rajahansa roared again and shook Parmver.

"What? It can't be my father's fault," Haidar said.

Liander staggered into the hall and dropped to his knees. "The king and queen, they're gone." He gasped and then fell face first onto the golden floor.

Haidar released Tana and ran to his side, turning him over, feeling for a pulse.

"He's not dead." Parmver's scratchy voice whispered through the chamber. "He's just sleeping. Hard. He'll wake in about six hours."

Haidar jumped to his feet and came after Tana. "You poisoned him." He shook Tana as roughly as Rajahansa had been shaking Parmver.

The rough handling made Tana's head hurt even worse. Though the singing stone had slipped out of range, her fever still raged. She gasped and sagged in his grip.

"It wasn't her," Parmver said louder. "She knew nothing of it. Do you think an ignorant, uneducated girl from the jungle village could have planned this? I'm insulted. It was my doing, and mine alone. You three have acted disgracefully. I am the senior member of this household, and I taught you better than this. The bond between dragon and Naga is sacred. Rajahansa, you should be ashamed of yourself, treating Amar in this fashion. I should paddle all of your behinds and send you to bed without dinner. Did you think I would sit by and allow you to carry on this way? No. The stone is mine, and I summoned the sword to cut the king free. Tana is only an innocent pawn in this sick game, and—"

Rajahansa tightened his grip on Parmver, puncturing Parmver's chest with his claw, pressing it clear through his body so blood and gore ran between the gold dragon's fingers.

Haidar froze. Tana stopped breathing.

Rajahansa dropped Parmver's body and padded over to Tana and Haidar, leaving bloody claw prints across the golden floor. Rajahansa's dragonstone flashed.

Haidar raised a hand. "I can't . . . I still can't hear you."

Rajahansa roared again.

Haidar sucked in a sharp breath. "Amar . . . Amar has the stone, and as long as he keeps it loose, you can't communicate, you can't use your power?"

Rajahansa swiped Haidar and Tana aside and ran from the chamber to the one beyond where an open window waited. Roaring, he dove out of the palace toward the jungle below.

Biting her lip, Tana hoped Amar and Mani had reached the safety of the trees. She and Parmver had bought them as much time as possible. Tana choked back a sob. Parmver had paid for that time with his life. She staggered across the chamber to where Parmver had fallen. So much blood. His lifeless eyes stared up into her face, locked forever in a state of surprise and shock.

She closed them, drew his head onto her lap, and wept.

Haidar came over and knelt beside her, putting a hand on Parmver's arm. "Oh, father." His voice was raw with pain and sorrow. "Why couldn't you just stay in your chamber and read your books until this all passed like I told you to? You didn't need to do this. I promised you everything would be all right."

Tana wiped the sweat and tears from her eyes. "You call this all right?"

Haidar grabbed her arms. Moisture trickled from his eyes. "It was not supposed to go like this. Khalid promised us victory. He said no one would die."

Tana shook her head. Her fever made her dizzy, and she found it difficult to draw air into her lungs. "King Khalid, the tyrant of Stonefountain? He's dead. How could he promise you anything?"

"Tana, be silent, please. You don't know anything that's going on." Haidar rose and stepped away from her, but as he did, his hand brushed her forehead.

"You're hot." He jerked her to her feet and pressed his hand against her cheek. "How long. How long have you had this fever? Tell me. You could not be so hot if you barely came down with it since I checked this morning."

Tana gave in. It was useless to try and hide it from him now. "Since you banished Kanvar's dragon from the palace. Parmver was giving me herbs to keep the fever down."

Haidar looked pained. "By the fountain, why, old man, why?"

"Perhaps he did not approve of you forcing me to marry you." Tana stepped away from Haidar. With Kanvar banished, Devaj run away, the king gone, and Parmver dead, there was nothing to keep Haidar from doing anything he wanted to her. She wished she had another singing stone to at least keep him out of her mind.

Haidar's face grew red with anger. "This is not about what my father approves of or what you or I might want, it's about the survival of our race. That has to come first before anything else."

Tana gathered her dress in her hands. She needed to hold onto something, anything. She was down to only one last option to frustrate Haidar's plans for her—a crazy, dangerous option that would likely not work at all.

"Go to your room," Haidar ordered. "Dress yourself for the Bonding Ceremony. Your time has come. Do not fret so." He ran a finger down her cheek. "The Bonding

Ceremony is a time of joy. It feels good, believe me, to become whole, to have all the emptiness inside you filled, to overflow with power and belonging. Though you may fear me, you need not fear this ceremony."

Rajahansa's angry roar shivered the palace as he flew back into the adjoining chamber and stalked into the throne room. Leaves and vines clung to his claws where he had torn at the jungle canopy attempting to reach the king.

Tana smiled to herself. Since he did not have Amar with him, he must have failed.

In a mad fury, Rajahansa tore the gold from the columns in the room, picked up the throne and smashed it against the wall, then came over to Parmver's body and picked it up, shaking it again and again as if he could somehow make the old man go back in time and change what he'd done.

Haidar waited to speak until Rajahansa had ended his mad rant and slumped to the floor, panting. "Your Majesty. Tana has the dragon fever. She's far gone in it. Parmver has been giving her medicine for it for quite some time. I can't fathom why."

Rajahansa got to his feet and scratched a message with his claw on the golden floor. *This is not over. We will proceed as planned. Amar may evade me for a day, but not forever. Go. Gather the dragon's for the ceremony.*

Haidar nodded. "Go to your chambers, Tana. I will come for you in a moment."

"We must bury your father," Tana said. "He must have a proper funeral."

"We will, Tana, I promise. Leave that to me and the gold dragons. You, go and get ready." Haidar led her out of the room and sent her on her way.

Chapter Four

Tana fingered Liander's jungle knife as she gazed out of her chamber window. Far below her, the jungle teemed with life and the promise of safety. Her ceremonial robe shimmered golden in the sunlight. The cool breeze kissed her cheeks. The time had come. She stepped up on the windowsill, shuddered and stepped back down.

"Come on, Tana. You have to do this," she told herself. Her hands clenched in fear.

She climbed back up and held the knife out over the long drop. She needed the knife, but it would be too dangerous to carry it down with her in her hand. I just hope I can find it again when I get to the jungle, she thought as she let it slip through her fingers. It tumbled away, sunlight glinting off the blade as it fell—one second, two, five, ten, fifteen, sixteen. It vanished into the leaves of the canopy so far away that Tana could not even hear the slap of the knife against the leaves and branches.

She took a deep breath. Her muscles tensed.

"Stop!" Haidar's command froze her in place. "What are you doing?" He strode into the room and tore her down from the windowsill.

Tana's heart dropped, tumbling away like the knife. Her hesitation had cost her this perfect chance to escape.

Haidar wrapped one hand around the back of her head and pressed the other to her temples. "You will not kill yourself." It was a command backed with power that bored into the very core of her mind. He kissed her then, his lips gentle and soft, so unlike Liander's. He pulled away and caressed her hair. "You and I are meant to be together. I will make you happy. I promise."

Tana blinked back tears. Part of her wanted to believe him. Part of her wanted to love him. He was not young, but he did not look old. His skin was golden bronze, his hair like sunshine. His kiss ignited a longing in her she had not expected. But was it truly her longing, or just Haidar playing with her emotions? If he was using his power on her now, she had not sensed it.

"No, Haidar." She tried to push him away, but he held her. "I love Kanvar."

"Are you sure?" Haidar's mind slid into hers and turned over the memories of how Kanvar had betrayed her.

How Kanvar had held her in his arms and promised he would keep her secret and then had broken that promise as soon as she was out of his sight. Then Haidar twisted her thoughts to another truth she could not deny. Kanvar had ignored her as soon as she came to the palace to be with him. He'd left her without even looking back, so intent on his own course he'd brushed her aside. Kanvar had spent only a few moments with her in her whole life and almost none at all since she'd come to the palace.

"And who has been here for you?" Haidar said, brushing his fingers down her cheek and lifting her chin. "I have, every day asking after your welfare, seeing to your needs, showing you consideration and kindness. And who will be there for you forever, loving you no matter what? I will." He leaned down and kissed her again, gentle and short, leaving her wanting more. "Come, the gold dragons are assembled."

He led her from her chambers down to the great hall. Six wide, arched windows opened out on blue sky. Four main halls led off from the room. A golden sunburst accented the center of the floor. This was the place where dragons took off and landed regularly, where dragons and Nagas met together to celebrate and share their creations of poetry, story, and art, where ceremonies of great occasion took place.

Gold dragons filled the hall, staying back away from the center where Rajahansa presided over two lines of young female dragons. Six on one side and six across from them with a wide path between the two lines for Tana to walk. This was the formation of the Choosing Ceremony since Tana had not yet chosen which dragon to bond to, though she'd walked this path from Rajahansa down the line of dragons to the window and back more than once now. Perhaps this time there would be a dragon she was drawn to.

As she stepped up to where Rajahansa waited, she let her feelings go out to the young dragons, opening herself to their minds and emotions. She felt nothing, no longing, no peace, no wholeness. Her mind flitted to green moss, patterned in pictures, a cocoon of raw earth around her.

A Great Green dragon stirred in her mind. *Who are you?* it seemed to ask.

"Tana, you must curtsy," Haidar whispered sharply in her ear.

She realized Rajahansa had just bowed to her. She tried to curtsy, though her robe was a bit too awkward and stiff to make it look good. She wobbled a bit, and Haidar kept her from falling. He turned her to face him. "You must choose a dragon this time. If you don't, Rajahansa will choose for you and we will continue with the Bonding Ceremony with that choice. Do you understand me?"

Tana nodded. Fear and fever made her tremble.

"Just walk among them. Take your time. Touch their dragonstones and get to know them." Haidar gave her a nudge out between the dragons.

Tana took a deep breath and started down the left-hand set. Her robe rustled as she moved. She willed her hand to reach out to the dragons waiting there, but it remained clutched against her side. She did not need to touch them to feel them. They were cold to her, meaningless as statues. Her heart yearned for the jungle, the scent of rich earth and greenery, the vibrant orange and purple flowers, the cry of the black monkeys, the flutter of birds, the taste of orchid nectar on her tongue. There was life down in the jungle, abundant and endless. The thought of it throbbed in her chest in time with her slow steps along the line of dragons.

She stopped at the last dragon on this side and forced herself to reach out and stroke the dragon's stone. The dragon's mind burst forcefully into hers. Too strong. She snatched her hand back, shaking.

She turned to face Rajahansa. "I-I've made my choice," she said as she backed up toward the window. "Th-this dragon here." She pointed to the one she had touched. "Affonaly." An artist of tapestries, a weaver of fabric and designer of human gowns. It was a close enough match,

Haidar and Rajahansa might believe it at least for a moment, and a moment more was all she needed.

Rajahansa lowered his head in a gesture of acceptance. His dragonstone flashed. Tana wondered if his power to speak had returned yet.

"Very well," Haidar said. He waved for Liander to step forward. Liander came, carrying a golden chalice and a dagger. The king's sword that should have been there for the Bonding Ceremony had gone with Amar into the jungle. Haidar grimaced as he took the dagger and chalice from Liander's hands. Then he strode down the line of dragons toward Tana.

Tana backed away, up against the windowsill. "I-I don't want to be cut."

"You need not fear, Tana. It will only hurt for a moment," Haidar said, stopping in front of the dragon. "I'm sorry, Affonaly. This dagger will not cut so cleanly through your plates as the king's sword would have. Hold out your foreclaw."

Affonaly held out her foreclaw and Haidar slid the tip of the blade up beneath one of the plates and nicked her flesh, drawing blood. The dragon let out a small moan as her blood flowed into the chalice.

With all eyes on the dragon, the chalice, and the blood, Tana leaped up on the windowsill and dove into the open air beyond.

Her stomach curled into a ball as she fell. The wind slapped her face. She leaned into it, keeping her arms tight against her sides, forcing her head down and feet up to streamline her body and speed her fall.

How long until Rajahansa and the other dragons notice her gone from the window?

One second, two. And they could fly. They'd come after her.

Three seconds, four. The wind whipped her face, drawing her lips back in a grin, her braid flapped against her back.

Five seconds, six. Her arms shook from the effort of holding them in.

Seven.

Eight.

Rajahansa's roar echoed across the sky and the flap of wings sounded above her.

Nine.

Tana gritted her teeth. She could hear her heart beat above the scream of the wind rushing over her.

Ten.

She felt Rajahansa dive toward her. A dozen other dragons filled the sky.

Eleven.

She blocked their presence from her mind, all except Rajahansa. He bore down on her, readying his back claws to snatch her from her fall.

Twelve.

Tana snapped her arms and legs out and twisted to the side. The fabric she had sewn between the sleeves of the robe and the legs, and reinforced with wooden dowels to make a sort of wing, caught the wind, spinning her away from the spot Rajahansa's claws snapped to catch her.

Rajahansa roared.

Thirteen.

Tana pulled her arms back in to her sides, diving again for the canopy. It loomed close now, filling her sight—trees and leaves and flowers.

Fourteen.

Rajahansa snatched at her again, this time aiming where she'd be if she spread her arms again.

Instead of spreading her wings, Tana curled into a ball and rolled forward.

Fifteen.

Rajahansa's talons closed on empty air again.

Tana snapped her arms back out and pulled her head and shoulders up, flaring her wings just above the canopy.

Sixteen.

A flurry of small yellow birds screeched and took to the sky as Tana settled into the leafy fronds of the tree. Her descent slowed, she edged her arms halfway toward her body, so she could continue her fall down through the leaves, past the branches, toward the understory. Twigs slashed at her arms and face. Wet leaves slapped her.

Above, Rajahansa howled in rage and tore at the tree tops. But the trees were too dense for a winged majestic dragon his size to get through.

Tana reached out her hands and grabbed a tangle of vines, slowing her descent bit-by-bit to a stop. She dragged in a shaking breath and hung for a long moment above the jungle floor before letting herself slide the rest of the way down. As soon as her feet touched the mossy soil, she doubled over, gasping. She'd done it. Chills from the fever shook her.

Tana. Haidar's mind reached out to hers. She sensed his intent to stop her escape, to take control of her mind and body and force her to climb back to the top of the trees where he and his dragon could come for her. She flung up a shield between them, the best she could master from the training Parmver had given her, while she stripped the cumbersome robe off, rolled it in a bundle and tied it to her back. Beneath the robe, she'd worn her village clothes—a mottled green tunic and leggings spun from the down of seed pods. It leeched off the sweat that soaked her body, keeping her relatively dry, and let her blend in with the jungle foliage.

She looked around for the jungle knife. She knew she could survive in the jungle with just the knife, but it was nowhere in sight. A pity to loose such a magnificent steel blade, but she'd jumped from a different spot from where she'd dropped it. There was no chance of her finding it in the dense jungle, especially with Haidar trying to wrench control of her own mind away from her.

Giving up on the knife, she ran.

Chapter Five

Tana pushed palm fronds aside and squeezed between thin saplings. Tall grass and leaves rustled as she made her way through the dense undergrowth. It took a few minutes for her eyes to adjust to the deep jungle twilight down below the trees where little sun fell. She was glad to be back below the canopy, back in the sticky heat and the safety of the trees. This was her home, full of life and activity and danger. Small snakes and tiny lesser serpents in a rainbow of colors scurried away as she parted the underbrush. Swarms of midges filled the air with a gentle hum. Tana kept her mouth shut and breathed through her nose to keep them from flying into her mouth.

In the late afternoon, the black monkeys were silent, lolling quietly in the trees. The smaller ring-tailed monkeys sucked juice from fruit and tossed the green husks down on Tana's head as she passed. She hooted at them, and they scattered.

As soon as she felt the press of Haidar's mind ease up and leave her, Tana paused. Sweat trickled down her face. Though she was sweating, she felt cold. It had to be caused by the fever, for she knew the jungle was not cold. Fever aside, she had to concentrate now. She was a long way from the village, and racing heedlessly along the jungle floor would get her nowhere. She could walk in circles for days. The thick trees blocked out all frames of reference for navigation.

Her mouth felt cottony with thirst, her body losing so much moisture from the sweat, she would have to drink soon to replenish it. She fingered a vine that hung down beside her. If only she could have jumped a moment after the jungle knife, she could have had it with her and fresh water would only be a few slashes away.

She shook her head and rubbed the sweat out of her eyes. Concentrate. Think now, get fresh water later. Listen. The midges' hum, the indolent grunt of a black monkey, the call of birds, a chorus of frogs croaking, some fast, some slow, some with deep sonorous voices, others with bright trills. And beneath all this thrum of sound, the faintest gurgle to her left behind a thick stand of bamboo. She'd never get through the bamboo without a jungle knife, so she worked her way around it, pausing every few feet to listen again, to be sure she was heading in the right direction.

She came to a place where the bamboo thinned enough she could squeeze through it, though the wooden dowels in the robe on her back caught for a moment, and she had to shift it to move forward. There, on the other side of the bamboo, a trickle of water a hand-length wide made its way beneath the trees. A gray turtle crawled across the muddy streamlet and faded into the bushes on the other side.

Tana watched the water for a moment, noting the direction it flowed. Then she set off downstream. Using the waterway as a path, her passage through the undergrowth became easier. The mud squished up soft and cool beneath her feet.

She'd been unhappy on the day her father and the king had forced her to come to the palace. Even in flight she had stared down at the jungle, the joy of riding the gold dragon swallowed up in her desire to track the course of the flight so she could find her way back someday. From above the canopy, the jutting peaks and precipices made easy landmarks. All useless and invisible from the ground.

The feature that had seared into her mind was the river. The Black River, her people called it. The dragon flight had swept above its winding curves, following its snaking path from the village to the mountain where the water originated. She could not see or hear the river now, but water was attracted to water. The streamlet would lead her to a bigger stream which would lead into the river, and the river would take her home.

She swallowed the dry in her mouth and scanned the vegetation around her as she moved, noting the trees and vines. This one's sap could heal, that one's produce red dye for clothing, and that one's make baskets water tight or set a glossy finish on wood. Those long, thin branches half the size of her finger could be split and used as rope for lashing. Everything in the jungle had a use, even the little yellow and black frogs no bigger than her thumb whose skin secreted a toxic poison used to tip blow darts, darts deadly enough to kill a black monkey in its tracks. All these things she could access and use, but none of them without a jungle knife. Though the flight on the dragons had been swift, she knew she had a long way to go to reach home. Days at the fastest. She needed a knife to survive, and for that she needed the river.

She pressed on, though the rash on her chest started to itch, and breathing became more difficult, the air heavier and heavier.

She gasped, pausing to rest, watching for predators, listening for the sound of the river. There it was, faint, up ahead. Wiping the sweat out of her eyes, she pushed on. Thirsty. Determined.

The streamlet joined with two others and deepened so the water came up above her ankles. She was moving toward the sound of the river and happy for it. An hour later her trek ended with a sudden splash into turbid black water. She laughed, and treaded water, letting the current carry her downstream along the shoreline. Water ran in rivulets down her face and hair. The sacred Black River gave life to her people and would take her back to them. The river was deep here, undercutting root and soil as she swam along the edge until the river turned, leaving a spit of rock and sand on the inner side.

She climbed up onto the spit and sank to her knees. The river stretched in a loop around her, glittering like a black snake in the sunlight. She felt happy and at peace for the first time since Rajahansa had chained the king. With trembling fingers she searched the rocks for a large piece of obsidian. The river gurgled. The air rippled with heat. The shiny black rock was abundant here, and it didn't take her long to find a suitable piece.

She set to work on it, her hands moving quick and sure, using another rock to chip the obsidian at an angle. Let Nagas like Haidar and Liander have steel jungle knives. She would have better. The *tap tap tap* of rock on rock filled her with joy as she fashioned her own knife, sharp and black. She leaped to her feet when it was done, and ran along the strip toward the trees. It just needed a handle, and all the wealth of the jungle would be hers.

The air in front of her rippled, and Haidar's voice wrapped around her body and mind in a firm command. "Stop."

She froze, her heart twisting in fear.

Rock crunched as Haidar's dragon settled to the ground, only its tail visible as it snaked into the shade of the trees. Haidar slid off the dragon and walked over to her.

"I knew you'd come to the river."

"Let me go," Tana said.

"You know I'm not going to do that." Haidar rested a hand on her shoulder. "At least, not until after the bonding ceremony. I can see you want to go home to your people. Very well, you may go home . . . after you bond to the gold dragon Rajahansa has now chosen for you. To do anything else would be to throw your life away. You're far too beautiful and valuable for that."

Tana clenched her fists, the obsidian blade hot in her hand. "I don't want to bond to a gold dragon."

"Tana." Haidar pulled her close to him and kissed her forehead. "You're a Naga, whether you like it or not. You must bond with a gold dragon."

Tana recoiled.

"What?" Haidar gripped both her shoulders and looked hard into her eyes, into her mind.

Tana locked a wall around her sense of the Great Green dragon, which she carried as a part of herself, and amplified her feelings of disgust at Haidar's treatment of King Amar and Queen Mani. And more, she fed him her raw feelings of despair and alarm that he had stood by and watched his own father murdered. He not only let Raja-hansa kill the kind old man, he continued to follow the commands of the tyrant dragon even after. What kind of a man was Haidar? Cruel, manipulative, incapable of love.

Haidar's hand struck her face.

The blow whipped Tana's head back and startled her with pain. She would have expected such from Liander but not Haidar.

"I loved my father!" Haidar shouted and pushed her to the ground. "And I loved you. Would you blame a man for wanting to protect his home?"

"I blame a man for loving gold and stone more than flesh and blood, more than family and king. You are a monster!" Tana wiped the trickle of blood from her throbbing lip.

"Get up. Move." Haidar jerked her to her feet. "I don't care whether you love me or not. You are coming back to the palace. You will bond with a gold dragon, and you and I will rebirth the Naga race."

Haidar's order to move freed Tana's frozen feet. "I will never . . . marry . . . you!" She slashed the obsidian knife across Haidar's chest, raced around his dragon into the trees, and thrashed into the deep darkness of the jungle away from the river and its sure way home.

Despite Dharanidhar's shame, Kanvar and Devaj found him quite willing to drink the medicine Devaj had prepared for him. Kanvar had eaten a meal of fried fish and sour yellow fruit with the villagers.

Denali and Eska had not come yet and were back at the village helping others pack their belongings and make ready for the move. Karishi, it seemed, was refusing to move at all. He and Tazaran had already started to delve a new home for themselves in the mountain beside the village. Kanvar worried that Karishi's feelings lay more with Haidar and Liander. Taking their side, he would not abandon his home and intended to fight instead.

Kanvar tried to give words of encouragement to the villagers, but most were too stunned to respond. Jabari, Tana's father and village chieftain, was overseeing the building of new huts in a clearing at the edge of the jungle. After Kanvar's brief visit while waiting for Dharanidhar to rest while the medicine started to work, Jabari stopped Kanvar as he was making ready to leave. He had a troubled look on his sweat-streaked face.

"Kanvar, Devaj said this was all your fault, the human armies coming, us having to move."

Kanvar tensed. He had never imagined his brother would speak ill of him. Devaj had not made any indication he was angry with Kanvar before flying back to get the next load of villagers. "He . . . said that? Was he angry?"

Jabari shook his head and glanced across the sky in the direction Elkatran and Devaj had flown. "No. He seemed reluctant to say anything about you, but we pressed him. We have a right to know why our lives are in danger. Why we must leave behind everything we've known, all we've built, and come to this place. We demanded to know, and he said that you had gone to help the humans fight a fellow Naga, that you took the side of the humans and told them where our hidden village was. What he did not say, but I read thick in his silence, is that you asked the humans to come here so you could overthrow your father and take the throne and the palace for yourself. You are bound to the Great Blue dragon, and the blue dragons have always sought the overthrow of the Naga king. It was the humans and blue dragons that destroyed Stonefountain. I have had this overshadowing thought that you intend to finish the job with the death of King Amar, Parmver, and his family."

Consternation swept over Kanvar like the ocean waves lapping at the beach behind him. For a moment, he could not speak. Heat rose to his face. "I . . . I would never betray my father. That is not what is happening at all. Devaj must not have explained things very well."

"Did you help the humans?" Jabari snapped. The salty ocean breeze ruffled his feathered cloak.

Kanvar frowned and clenched his fist. "Yes."

"Against another Naga?"

"Yes, but no. I was trying to save the Naga and bring him back to the safety of the palace. It is not my fault the humans know about us. Devaj went to the Maran colony to find me. They've known there are Nagas in Kundiland since then. They could not help but react when some Naga tried to take over their world."

"What Naga would do such a thing?" Jabari's face had gone from troubled to livid.

"His name is Rajan. He's Kumar Raza's twin brother. But it wasn't his fault. A Great Red volcanic dragon was controlling him. Kumar Raza and I freed Rajan from the dragon, and they're on their way back here now." Kanvar wished his grandfather had already arrived. Kumar Raza would know better how to deal with Jabari's concerns.

Jabari's brow furrowed. "So, you are not trying to kill your father?"

"No. I'm trying to save him." Kanvar's mind spun, trying to decide how much he should tell Jabari about Khalid and Rajahansa's betrayal. Devaj had obviously not wished to divulge the inner workings at the Naga palace to Jabari and the villagers. It was a delicate matter. How could he explain the Gold Dragon King's betrayal of his lifelong friend and companion?

"Save him?" Jabari's voice rose. "You call setting a human army on him saving him?"

"No." Sweat trickled down the back of Kanvar's neck. "The humans would have come one way or another, sooner or later after seeing Devaj. It is only sooner because Rajan and the red dragon stirred them up. The problem is the dragons and Nagas at the palace had a disagreement about what should be done. Some—my father, Devaj, and I—wanted to evacuate along with you and your people. Others did not. They rebelled against the king and have taken him prisoner. They intend to stay and fight the humans. The truth is, the Great Blue dragon pride is doing all they can to keep King Amar safe."

Jabari took a deep breath and his troubled features smoothed. "Devaj did not mention any of that."

"Devaj did not want to burden you with Naga disputes."

"I don't know who to believe, you or your brother. I don't know what to think anymore." Jabari glanced over at his people, working hard to build new houses and settle a new village.

"I'm sorry you had to leave the village," Kanvar said. "But houses are replaceable. Human lives are not. Devaj and I just want to make sure everyone gets to safety."

"I suppose so." Jabari clapped Kanvar on the shoulder and then strode back to help with the building.

Kanvar tried to shake off the foreboding their conversation had caused to come over him. He reached Dharanidhar's side and let his friend hoist him onto his back. Once Kanvar was buckled, Dharanidhar took to the air. He felt better. The medicine did help. They flew south. Sometime later, they found a sheltered cover ringed by cliffs much like the nesting grounds the blue dragons had once lived in on the east coast. It was sheltered on all sides and hidden by a headland that wrapped a concealing arm around the beach and cliffs. Dharanidhar landed on the fine black sand and let out a contented purr.

Chapter Six

Huddled in a dense part of the jungle where she figured Haidar would never come and his dragon would not be able to reach, Tana fashioned a wooden handle for her knife then lashed the two together. Thoughts of what she'd done plagued her. How easily human skin cut beneath her hand. How angry Haidar must be at her. She needn't worry now that he still wanted her, need she?

By the time she finished making her jungle knife, nightfall was imminent.

She pushed the thoughts of Haidar aside, only to have them replaced with memories of Parmver. The old man had been so kind and patient with her as he tried to teach her to read and about what it meant to be a Naga. He couldn't be dead. He just couldn't be.

She brushed a tear from her cheek and set up camp for the night, hacking a section free of underbrush that could shelter unwanted creatures and sweeping it aside. By cutting saplings, lashing them together, and covering over the top of them with palm fronds, she built herself a raised shelter. Using her knife, she stripped long pieces of bark from the wood and fashioned a hammock, which she hung beneath the shelter.

She got it up just before the rain started. Here was water aplenty to quench her thirst. She need only hold out a large leaf, let the water pool in it, then bend the edges up and tip the water into her mouth. Real water, tasting of jungle green, not cold iced water from the palace.

She chopped a small palm tree down and peeled off the outer layers of bark and wood to get to the heart. The crisp meat of the tree made her mouth water and filled her belly. After she'd eaten, she crawled into her hammock and listened to the patter of the rain against the palm fronds over her head.

Her fever made her dizzy, and the rash on her chest would not stop itching. In the morning she'd have to find a dragon's blood tree and harvest the sap to stop the itch. If she lived until morning. All the Nagas insisted she would die if she did not bond. Without Parmver's medicines, her symptoms had grown worse.

Her heart twinged. How could Rajahansa have killed him without even a second thought? All her life she and the other villagers had worshipped the Great Gold Dragon King. Rajahansa was their protector. She could not wrap her mind around what she'd seen at the palace. Everything she'd ever been taught about the Nagas seemed to be a lie. And not. King Amar had treated her with love and respect as if she'd been his own daughter. Mani and Eska had welcomed her as a friend and fellow woman. Devaj had been gallant, gentle, and kind. Karishi had shown a noble interest in her, but deferred to Devaj as the king's heir. The Naga palace was like a tree split by lightning, the two sides riven from each other by Kanvar's actions.

Kanvar. Tana sighed and twirled the jungle knife in her hands. She'd been attracted to him from the moment she first saw him standing down a crazed Great Green dragon. There had been something about the way he carried himself, a confidence, no . . . defiance, coupled with a tinge of hurt in his eyes as if the whole world were a ferocious green dragon set on devouring him. And he faced it with an imperfect body—his stumpy left arm and twisted left leg that some people in the village found revolting, but Tana found compelling. Kanvar was a man who was different from others by his very physical being. And that physicality had produced in him a solid steel core, making him a man of courage, a man of action, a man willing to fight for what he believed in.

Yes, Kanvar was the lightning that had shivered the Naga tree from crown to root. Many trees struck by lightning died. Some survived. This one, it seemed, would never be whole again. Two Nagas and their dragons stood on one side: Haidar and Liander. Two Nagas and their dragons stood on the other: Devaj and Kanvar. Karishi had fled into the mountain by the village to avoid conflict. Parmver had stood in the middle and died. The kings, Rajahansa and Amar, were split right down the center of their link with each other. Would that the separation could somehow be healed, but Tana could not imagine how.

She worried for Amar and Mani, stumbling around somewhere on the jungle floor. Perhaps she shouldn't. King Amar had taken his equipment with him, and he knew how to survive in the jungle. What intelligent creature would dare hurt him? And with his powers he could control all the wild creatures—if he used his powers. He could not while the singing stone was free from its iron box; Tana was sure of that. Yet, without the stone he could not have escaped. She sent her feelings out, trying to sense the singing stone. With such a shrill scream, if it were free from its box and anywhere close it should cut through her sense of teaming life in the jungle around her. She felt a familiar comforting presence instead.

Who are you? The question came as an impression to Tana's mind that was deeper than words and carried with it the presence of green and colored moss.

My name is Tana, she said, sending her thoughts out in return to the Great Green dragon who seemed to be a part of her . . . and not . . . yet.

Confusion came back from the dragon. It could not understand her.

I'm a Naga, Tana thought to the dragon, speaking with impressions and images as well as words. *I'm a Naga, and I need you. We should be together. I do not like the gold dragons. They fly above the jungle instead of living in its heart. I need heat and moisture and leaves and trees and living things all around me. Will you not be my dragon?*

Tana wished she could reach out and touch the Great Green dragon's stone so they could see fully into each other's minds and hearts. That would be a Choosing Ceremony worth attending.

A Naga? From the village? Fear, consternation, and a biting sadness emanated from the dragon.

Yes. Tana shared images of her hut in the village with the she-dragon.

My mate went in search of a Naga to bring to the king and was murdered for his effort. The corpse of the Great Green dragon Kanvar shot in Tana's defense sprang into Tana's mind.

Tana gasped and swung out of the hammock, landing on her feet, her knife clutched in her hand. *No, no. That can't be. The dragon was trying to paralyze me and take me back to his lair to eat me. He attacked me. I ran—who wouldn't run?—and Kanvar shot him to save me.* Tana replayed the events from her memories for the she-dragon, knowing the dragon could not hear her words but hoping the impressions would be clear enough to express Tana's shock and regret.

The Great Green she-dragon wept. *I told him not to go.*

Tana gritted her teeth. The rain continued in a torrent beyond the edge of her shelter. The last glimmer of light had vanished, leaving only darkness. Intending to sleep, Tana had not bothered to light a fire. Now she wished she had. Sleep had fled from her. She needed this dragon, a dragon of her own choosing to bond with. Not the golds. Not the sunlight and high places. Not their books and fancy clothes. She shivered.

I will die if I do not bond, she thought. *Tell me how to get to your lair. Forgive me for the death of your mate. Please. I wish death on no Great dragon, and Kanvar . . . he acts before thinking. Never considers the consequences. You are not the only one who has been hurt by his actions.* Tana shared a picture from her mind of Amar chained in his chamber, of Parmver lying dead on the floor. *But he does not mean for these things to happen. His heart is good. He just does what he thinks is right to save other people even if it means risking his own life.*

The green dragon snorted, called her yearlings up onto her back, and slithered out of her lair. *Stay put, Naga. I can feel your mind. I will come find you.*

No. The jungle by the palace is not safe. Haidar and Rajahansa seek to control all Great and lesser dragons here. They are gathering an army. The blue dragons may have dispersed it, but the Nagas are rebuilding it. If you come close, you'll be bound by their power and forced to fight the humans.

Tana stood at the edge of her shelter, wishing she could plunge into the darkness and race out to meet the she-dragon. But that would be sure death, blundering through the jungle in the dark.

Dragonbound VI

But I can see in the dark, the dragon said. *Be still. The other Nagas cannot trap my mind if I'm bound to you, can they?*

I don't know. They are much stronger than I am.

Be still. Wait.

I hate waiting. Tana paced back and forth across the short length of her shelter swinging her knife, biting her lip, and scratching her itchy chest. Sometime in the night, the rain stopped and the jungle came to life with noise. Frogs and insects filled the air with their song, a sweeter song than Parmver's singing stone, and yet the noise set Tana on edge.

She thought of the imminent attack by the humans. Would they come to the village first? Could they find it? Her father was there and all her friends. Perhaps Haidar was right to raise an army. This was Kundiland, the Dragon Lands. If the humans came here to invade, shouldn't they be met by dragons willing to fight? Perhaps Parmver was right and Haidar should try to defend his home. But not chain the king. Not hurt Mani's mind. Not let Rajahansa kill his father. These things were wrong. If only they had let Kanvar and his dragon come back to the palace. Kanvar knew more about fighting than they did. Kanvar was a survivor, but that had not turned him mean. He would never hit Tana, force her against her will, or destroy her mind. Surely a person could defend a home without turning evil.

Kanvar. Tana reached out with her mind, searching for his presence in the darkness. Her ability to sense things was still weak and unfocused. Parmver had said it would come more easily once she'd bonded. At least he'd taught her how to shield her mind from all the jungle creatures that had pressed in on her thoughts before. She could think as herself now and focus that self out to others. *Kanvar*, she called again. His mind was strong. Surely he could hear her, if he were close enough to the palace.

Tana? Kanvar's answer was faint and far away, like the last sighing of the wind across the edge of the jungle. The Great Green she-dragon had been closer, her thoughts clearer.

Kanvar, I've escaped the palace.

And my father?

I helped him and your mother escape as well. But I don't know where they are. We got separated. Tana shuddered and slumped back into her hammock. Trying to communicate with her thoughts added a sharp headache to her dizziness.

Your voice is fuzzy. I'm only getting faint impressions, Kanvar said.

I haven't bonded yet . . . but soon.

You've left the palace, how will you bond?

I don't like the gold dragons. They make me sick. My dragon is coming to me. A Great Green dragon. I have felt her as a part of me for a long time. At least Kanvar would understand about Tana rejecting the gold dragons. He had done the same. And they hated him for it. *Let them hate me,* Tana thought. *I don't care.*

A lilt of laughter from Kanvar tickled her mind. *I'll come help you with the bonding.*

No. I'm too close to the palace and too deep under the canopy. You can't reach me.

But my father is close. Did you say that? Did I feel that right? If he is, you should call him. He can help.

He has Parmver's singing stone. I cannot feel him. If he still has the stone out, he won't hear my thoughts. Tana rubbed her head. The pain was too much to continue her conversation with Kanvar. She let the connection drop. But Haidar's mind stabbed into hers in Kanvar's place.

Tana, you will pay for what you did to me. I'll be scarred for life because of you. Haidar wrapped his mind around hers and jerked her to her feet. *Come back to the palace now. I will meet you on the cliff steps up to my father's lab.*

Tana gasped and wrenched her mind away from Haidar. But his compulsion still dragged her out of her shelter into the rain.

Leave her alone. Kanvar's command severed Haidar's control over her. She sensed Haidar and Kanvar's minds struggling with each other, neither prevailing, both too far away from each other to have much effect other than to free Tana. She ducked back under the shelter and rebuilt the shields around her mind. Calling Kanvar must have given her position away to Haidar. She vowed not to make that mistake again if she could help it.

Something moved out in the jungle. A rustling and snapping sound silenced the frogs. It drew closer, and the sound resolved into a familiar refrain, the tap and swish of a jungle knife hacking through underbrush and the muted steps of humans moving beneath the trees.

Tana readied her knife and waited. Could Haidar really be angry enough at her to venture down to the jungle floor in the dark? She strained to see the glow of a lantern in the direction of the sound. Surely no one would pass through the darkness of the jungle at night without some form of illumination. All she saw was black upon black. She would have moved into deeper shadows to hide, but the darkness was already complete everywhere.

Her breathing seemed too loud in her ears, as loud as the hack and swish of the jungle knife.

Chapter Seven

"**T**ana," **a male voice** called out. "Tana, say something so I can find you."

It was King Amar. Tana let out a sigh and lowered her knife. She wished she could lower her shields so she could sense his presence out there in the dark, but no. Haidar would find her mind again. She had to be careful.

"Your Majesty," she said. Her voice sounded small in the vastness of the night though she tried to project so he could hear her. "This way, Your Majesty. Are you all right? Is the queen well?"

"We're alive. Keep talking."

The king must have felt her mind as well as Haidar when she'd reached out to Kanvar, felt it and left the safety of his own camp to come to her. Crazy. But with the stone put away he could protect himself from any animal with his mind.

"I'm this way. I have shelter, but no fire, no light. I should have made one before it started raining, but I didn't." She rambled on as the jungle knife strokes came closer and then stopped as shuffled footsteps approached the shelter.

"Tana?" Amar's voice was soft and reassuring.

"Here, Your Majesty."

The king's arms caught her up in a fatherly hug. "Tana, my dear, sweet child." He pressed her against his chest. His cool dragonscale armor felt smooth against her cheek. "You risked so much to free us. How can I ever repay you?"

Tana's throat constricted. "Parmver has already paid with his life."

"What?" Amar's voice was as raw as a sharpening stone, rasping against a knife blade.

"Rajahansa and Haidar were about to blame me for your escape, but Parmver claimed all the credit for it. He chided Rajahansa for what he'd done to you and . . . Rajahansa just . . . killed him." This close and touching the king, Tana's memories of the horror of Parmver's death seeped through both their shields into Amar's mind.

Amar cried out and pulled away from Tana, dropping his jungle knife, and falling to his knees. "He didn't. He couldn't. He's gentle and respects all living things. Strict maybe, yes he's strict, but not a murderer, not this. I am not a murderer."

A dress rustled as Mani knelt down beside her husband and lifted his supply pack and crossbow from his back. "Amar, listen to me. Your dragon's actions are not your own. You did not kill Parmver."

"We are one. We are the same. He is me and I am him."

Tana could not see the tears on the king's face, but she could hear them in the sob of his voice.

"No." Mani's words were as gentle as if comforting a child. "I was wearing the singing stone. Your minds were blocked from each other, separate. You have no responsibility for Rajahansa's actions."

Amar moaned and crumpled to the ground, curling into a ball.

Tana set her knife down next to the corner pole of the shelter where she could find it again and went to the king. "Your Majesty. You can't lie on the ground. I've cleared it, but there could still be termites, stinging ants, and scorpions. Come. There's a hammock. Mani, help me get him into it."

With Mani's help, Tana coaxed the stricken king from the ground and eased him into the hammock. Amar's breathing was ragged and shallow, his muscles tense. After Tana was sure the king was secure in the hammock, she backed a step away. Mani stayed beside him, a comforting hand on his shoulder.

"What's wrong, my love?" Mani said. "Has Rajahansa woken? Shall I get the stone out again?"

Amar whimpered.

Tana sensed the weight and power of Rajahansa's mind wrestling with Amar's.

"Khalid!" Amar cried out.

Mani jerked back, pulled the iron box from her pocket, and opened the lid. The blue glow of the stone lit up the shelter, casting a ghostly hue on Amar's gaunt face. His cry of pain intertwined with the wail from the stone.

Tana pressed her hands against her ears, but it did no good. She heard the scream of the singing stone with her mind, not her body.

Amar shivered in pain for a moment then fell unconscious. Mani snapped the lid closed, and the ghostly light vanished. "The stone hurts him," she said.

Tana nodded and sucked in a ragged breath. To say the stone hurts was an understatement. "I only hope it hurts Rajahansa just as much. He's the one who deserves the pain." Tana blinked the spots from her eyes left from the stone's light.

"I don't like Amar calling out that name. Khalid the Tyrant died a thousand years ago," Mani said.

"Why would he call for Khalid, if Khalid is dead?" Tana retrieved her jungle knife and set to work stripping more bark from the poles she'd used to build the shelter.

Her hands shook, making it hard to work. Her mind felt like it too had been stripped clean of bark.

"Amar told me that Rajahansa sent Devaj to Stone-fountain." Mani wiped the sweat from her husband's brow. "Khalid's spirit attacked Devaj from the fountain and tried to possess him. Kumar Raza pulled him out of there, but Khalid had formed some kind of a link with Devaj's mind. Amar told me he was keeping Devaj's mind shielded from Khalid. If Amar is now sensing Khalid in Rajahansa's mind, this does not bode well. Amar insists Rajahansa's actions are not normal, but I believe they are in line with what we know of Khalid."

Tana wove the strips of bark together with practiced fingers while Mani talked. Tana's heart seemed to tighten with the strands of the hammock she was making. She did not know much of this ancient king, Khalid. The stories her people told said only that he was evil and had ruled the old world. His power and cruelty had never reached into the depths of the jungle to strangle her people, until now. "You think Khalid has taken over Rajahansa's mind?"

"I don't know. Perhaps not taken over—Rajahansa is more powerful than Devaj—but influenced, certainly. Or so it would seem. I don't like it." Mani felt through the darkness to find Tana and clutched her hands. "And I don't like the dark. Don't your people have some way of making fire?"

"Not at the moment, My Queen." Tana pulled away gently and hung the hammock she'd been making. "If I had gathered the necessary things and started it before dark, we would have fire now. But, you'll be safe enough. I've made a bed for you too. Here, climb in and get some rest. I'll keep watch."

Tana helped Mani into the hammock and went back to pacing along the edge of the shelter, listening for danger from the jungle. The frogs returned to their song: the deep rhythmic thrum of the tumbler toads bearing up the constant beat of the tree frogs and the high counterpoint chirp of the dart frogs. The crickets and cicadas filled the air with their own buzz. Water, left from the rainstorm, dripped from leaf to leaf in a gentle uneven patter as it made its way down from the top layers of the canopy to the jungle floor. These were the sounds of jungle life, her life, her home, sounds she'd listened to every night, sounds that should bring her comfort, and yet they did not. Her chest burned and itched, leaving her antsy and uncomfortable.

The smell of fresh rain on the leaves promised a new day to come with first light, and Tana waited for that light, looking up to the treetops for the faint green glow that would signal the rising sun, imagining that she would wake with it and know this was all a dream. She had never gone hunting with Kanvar. Never left the village to go to the palace. Never faced Haidar and Liander. Never witnessed Parmver's murder. If only. She dozed, and when the light did trickle through the trees to rest on her, she woke and found a black monkey not a yard from her shelter. It was a large male, with black scales on its belly and thick fur down its back and arms. Its black eyes glittered as they stared at her, looked right into her as if it had been doing that for hours. Motionless. Just looking.

Tana jerked away from the pole she'd been leaning on and raised her knife.

The black monkey bared its sharp white teeth and growled at her, but did not back off. Strange behavior for a black monkey. They seldom confronted an armed human, only attacking weak and helpless humans, and only as a whole troop, not singly.

Tana glanced to the trees and listened for more of the monkeys, but saw and heard nothing. The male was alone.

"Get out of here!" she yelled and waved the knife. But the monkey remained frozen in place, its eyes never moving off of her, its tail not even twitching. Odd. Black monkey tails were always moving. It was like someone had set a statue of a monkey down right outside her shelter. Someone . . . Haidar.

Tana stared into the monkey's eyes and felt Haidar staring back at her. She leaped forward and thrust her jungle knife through the monkey's heart. Haidar's yelp of surprise and pain managed to make it past her shields.

Someday you're going to learn not to mess with me, Tana said, then thickened the shields around her mind, blocking it off from Haidar's. She pulled the knife free from the monkey, and it slumped dead at her feet.

When she turned away from it, she noticed Mani sitting up in the hammock staring wide-eyed at her.

"Breakfast," Tana said, gesturing toward the dead monkey. "It's time to light that fire."

King Amar stirred in his hammock, rubbed his eyes, and moaned.

"Morning, Your Majesty," Tana said. She found a dead sapling that stood next to her shelter, chopped it down with two swipes of her knife, and peeled the bark off to get to the dry wood beneath. She feathered the dry wood by scraping the edge of her knife down a length of it several times, then cut off the feather to use for kindling. She cut forearm-length pieces for the fire itself. Now she just needed tinder to get the fire started. Not a problem. Several trees in the jungle dropped seedpods full of fluffy down.

"Tana, where are you going?" Amar asked as she stepped away from the shelter to collect the pods. His voice was dry and scratchy. Dark circles hung under his eyes. His face was pale. Worse, he was no longer sweating. A body not slicked with sweat in the jungle was one dehydrated and in danger of heat sickness.

"Not far." She picked up a couple of seedpods from the base of a tree next to the shelter. "Are you thirsty, Your Majesty?" she asked as she cracked open the pods and extracted the fluff.

"What does it matter?" Amar said. "The weaker I get, the weaker it makes him. And believe me, weaker is better. We should probably get the singing stone back out, but I . . ." He rubbed his head.

"Is Rajahansa awake?" Tana asked. A few taps of a rock against the blade of her jungle knife sent sparks into the fluff, igniting a warm glow. She lifted the fluff and blew gently on it until flames licked her fingers. She set it down and lay the kindling on top of it, and the fire came to life.

"Yes." Amar let out a pained breath.

"Can he control you?" Tana fed the fuel wood into the fire and went to skin the black monkey.

"No. We're too well matched. I'd be in trouble if Haidar or Liander joined with him, but they seem to be busy with something else."

Tana glanced from the dead monkey in her hands to Amar, still couched in his hammock. "Imagine that. They're watching us and planning something, I'm sure. The question is what?"

"I don't want to know." Mani looked away as Tana cleaned and skinned the monkey. "I just want to find somewhere safe."

"We're a long way from safe." Amar wiggled out of his hammock and stood on shaking legs. "Give me the stone, Mani."

"No." Mani pressed her hand against the box in her pocket. "You're using it to purposely hurt yourself. If he can't control you, and he's not trying to control me, there is no reason to bring it out."

Tana set the haunches to cook over the fire, wiped the blood off her hands using a wet leaf, and went to Mani's side. "Mani is right, Your Majesty. You're too weak already. You need to eat and drink. Then we can move farther away from the palace. Punishing yourself with the stone won't bring Parmver back."

Amar licked his lips like he might say something in argument, but turned his back on them instead and ran his hand through his slack golden hair. The dappled sunlight glowed across the green dragonscale armor he wore. It was fine armor, and Tana liked it on the king better than all the golden robes he'd worn at the palace. He had the sword buckled at his side, and the golden hilt looked natural beneath the gauntleted hand he rested on it.

Tana picked up the king's jungle knife and set it on his pack, which was already crawling with ants. She should have hung the pack up when he arrived but hadn't thought to do it in the dead of night. His crossbow and harness with a dozen bolts leaned against the pack, a beautiful weapon, fit for a king.

The smell of blood and cooking meat drifted up in a cloud of smoke from the fire. Tana's stomach grumbled. Breakfast would be good.

A flash of green moved at the corner of her eye. She turned and saw a constrictor snake longer than the length of her shelter circling its way down the closest tree. A flock of small gray birds that had been pecking at the mushrooms in the trees burst into flight, heading for the top of the canopy. A lesser serpent with orange and black diamonds on its back scuttled out of the brush. Somewhere behind it, a larger serpent roared. The jungle came alive with dozens of snakes, serpents, and dragons, closing in on the campsite.

Chapter Eight

"Your Majesty," Tana said, readying her jungle knife. "I think I figured out what Haidar is up to. Mani, I think you should get out the stone."

King Amar whipped around and stared out at the approaching predators. "No wait," he told Mani. "They're hungry. It feels like Haidar hasn't been letting them eat. They smell the monkey's blood. It won't matter if we break Haidar's hold on them or not. They'll still attack, and if the stone is out, we won't be able to defend ourselves. Here, Mani." He snatched up the crossbow and pressed it into Mani's hands then drew his sword. "Tana." He nodded toward his steel jungle knife.

She snatched it up in her other hand so she had a knife in either hand, ready to use if attacked.

"We can't fight this many of them," Mani cried, but she released a bolt at the constrictor which had worked its way out of the tree and started into the shelter. The bolt went through the head, pinning the snake to the ground. It tried to hiss then gurgled, fell silent, and stopped moving. By the time it twitched its last, Mani had the crossbow reloaded.

"We shouldn't have to," Tana said. "You're Majesty, can't you control them? Send them somewhere else to feed."

Amar scoffed. "Rajahansa is blocking my powers."

"But why would he? He can't want you dead."

Six yellow-belly raptors rushed from the trees into the shelter. A seventh jumped from above, landing on top of the shelter and using its hooked claws to tear aside the leaves, and sharp teeth to snap the sticks that stood between it and the humans. Though the yellow-bellies were only knee high, they moved fast. Tana cut one down with the knife in her right hand and knocked one down with the knife in her left. A third sank its teeth into her leg before she could slice off its head. Mani hit the one on the roof with a crossbow bolt, and Amar killed two with one swing of his sword.

Even as the pack of raptors fell, other serpents rushed into the shelter, pressing Amar, Mani, and Tana out of the far side.

The orange and black serpent climbed up one of the poles and tried to spit its poison in Tana's eyes. She scrambled backward, unable to kill it and dodge the poison at the same time.

"Rajahansa, what are you doing?" Amar cried while stabbing a gray bark dragon that stood as tall as his shoulder.

Tana shook her head. Haidar was angry at her, but was he really angry enough to kill Amar too? Rajahansa would die if Amar did. Surely he would not let Haidar kill him.

A troop of black monkeys scrambled down from the trees and tore the shelter apart.

"This way." Amar grabbed his pack, motioned for Mani and Tana to follow him, and rushed out of the broken shelter into the trees on the far side.

Tana's golden Bonding Ceremony robe, the wings she had worked so hard on, fell to the ground as the shelter tumbled apart. With a knife in both hands, she could not retrieve it. She slashed at the orange and black serpent that came at her again from the ground now.

"Tana, come on," Amar called.

Tana threw her obsidian knife at the serpent, cutting off its head, snatched up her robe, and ran limping to join the king, wishing that the thick underbrush would be more of a protection for them than an advantage to their attackers, but knowing it wasn't.

More dragons and snakes pressed in on them from three sides, driving them backwards.

"Tana, use the jungle knife to cut us a path," Amar said. "Mani and I will keep these monsters at bay."

Tana turned and started cutting a clear escape but stopped after a few swipes and turned back.

"What are you doing?" Amar shouted as he killed a lesser green dragon that leaped from a tree and glided toward him.

"Rajahansa doesn't want you dead," Tana said. "The dragons aren't trying to kill us; they're driving us toward the river where the gold dragons can reach us."

A black monkey jumped on her head, wrapped its hands around her neck and bit at her face. She tried to throw it off, but three more joined the first, pinning her arms and legs. A fifth monkey landed on top of her, driving her to the ground. Grass and leaves rustled and slapped her in the face as the monkeys dragged her toward the river.

Amar shouted and his sword flashed, killing two of the monkeys that held her.

A dozen more monkeys bounded from the trees, swarming over Amar. A constrictor rose up out of the grass and got its coils around Mani.

Tana thrashed and swiped with her knife, trying to free herself from the monkeys. The salty taste of sweat and fear seeped into her mouth. The cut on her leg throbbed, and the monkeys' strong hands bruised her as she pulled away from them. She jumped to her feet, ran a step toward Mani, and splashed into a stream up to her knees.

The slimy coils of a lesser black serpent enveloped her. Its fangs snapped toward her neck. She barely had time to block the bite with her knife and hack off the serpent's head. She gasped for breath as the coils slid off her.

Shaking, she jumped out of the stream and hacked at the constrictor that had Mani bound. How could they survive this? What choice did they have but to retreat to the river?

The monkeys were all over Amar. Mani couldn't shoot them with the crossbow and Tana didn't dare swing at them with her jungle knife for fear of hitting him.

Tana's muscles burned with the exertion of swinging the knife as another pack of raptors, these ones black with red stripes on their faces and back, skittered out of the bushes and rushed her. The scent of blood and death enveloped her. The strident cry of the attacking black monkeys and the hiss of angry serpents filled the air.

The guttural roar of a Great dragon shook the trees.

The black monkeys froze. The raptors paused in their attack and cocked their heads, listening. The jungle fell silent for a breath until the Great dragon roared again. It was not the trumpeting call of a gold dragon. The voice was deep and earthy and held unbridled fury.

There are many dangerous creatures in the jungle, and none as dangerous as a Great Green dragon. The Great Greens were the largest of the jungle dragons, the most feared, and the most deadly. Though generally passive unless hunting, and that done quietly, the Great Green dragons were capable of unheralded violence, especially if their lair or young were threatened.

Tana smiled. All creatures of the jungle, no matter how hungry, would run from an angry Great Green.

The Great Green dragon roared again, but instead of running, the black monkeys and raptors redoubled their attack.

Tana yelled in frustration as she tried to keep the swarming raptors from tearing into her. Haidar's control of his dragon army kept them lashing out against the humans. "Mani, get out the singing stone," Tana called. "Do it now."

But Mani's hands were full, one with the crossbow she used as a club against a raptor that dropped toward her from a tree above, and the other with a bolt she used to impale a thin, brown running serpent.

Saplings thrashed and cracked as the Great Green dragon sped toward them.

Tana's heart rose up in her throat. She'd faced a Great Green dragon before. It had terrified her. The male dragon was stealth, cunning, and patience. Not so for the dragon that came for her now.

The she-dragon was power and fury.

Amar got free from the monkeys and raced to Mani's side. "Run," he cried, getting his arm around her and urging her down the stream toward the river. "I don't want to have to kill a Great Green."

"No wait!" Tana stood her ground even as a swarm of yellow snakes coiled down the trees toward her. She dispatched the last red and black raptor.

"Tana, it's a Great Green she-dragon. They only howl like that when someone has threatened their young. If

Haidar's convinced her we've done that, there will be no stopping her. I'd rather face the gold dragons than an angry mother green."

A laugh burst from Tana, bubbling out in a mix of exuberance and joy. Her sense of self joined with the Great Green she-dragon. The damp ground gave beneath her claws as she ran. Leaves flicked across her face and vanished behind her. Her wyrmlings clung to her back, their heads nestled against her spine. She smelled blood and knew her enemies were close. So many black monkeys and snakes, serpents and dragons, all attacking her last child. How dare they? Did they not know she ruled the jungle? She roared and the trees shook. Then she was upon the scene of carnage. She whipped her tail out in front of her, sliding it against a troop of black monkeys. They fell, paralyzed even as she pounced on a pair of red-striped raptors. Their bodies snapped like twigs in her jaws, their blood flowed across her tongue like sweet nectar. She clawed a constrictor snake and two green serpents to the ground. But the rest of the pack of raptors, who usually fled before her, redoubled the attack on the human man and woman and the girl-woman-child-her-wyrmling.

She devoured the raptors one by one, then monkeys, and every other creature that moved toward those she protected, until the jungle fell silent and the scent of blood overpowered the smell of green and growing things. Then nothing moved. The humans stood silent.

A man's voice cracked across her mind. *Great Green dragon, you are mine. You will obey my command. Drive the humans to the river.*

No, the girl-woman-child-her-wyrmling replied from inside her head. *The green dragon is mine.*

Tana built a shield around the Great Green dragon's mind and then separated herself from it, returning her thoughts to her own body. She found herself breathing hard and shaking with excitement. She'd been a dragon . . . for a moment. Her feelings, her thoughts, every sensation had been all dragon and filled her with power and freedom like a rush of whitewater roaring down a waterfall.

The Great Green she-dragon splashed across the stream to stand in front of Tana. It lowered its head, and Tana reached out a shaking hand to place on the dragonstone. The green stone was cool and sent tingles of power up her arm. The dragon's memories sank into her own. She was Vasanti, and the jungle was her home.

I am Tana, Tana answered in return. *And the jungle is my home as well.*

And this was how the Choosing Ceremony was supposed to be—both sharing memories and feelings, both their lives and minds wrapping up into one whole being. Peace settled over Tana like mist hugging the jungle ground in the morning.

"Tana." Amar's voice and gentle touch on her arm pulled her away from Vasanti.

Tana lowered her hand from Vasanti's dragonstone and turned to face the king.

"Good morning, Vasanti," Amar said to the dragon. "Your wyrmlings have grown much since I helped you hatch them."

Your Majesty. Vasanti bowed to Amar.

Tana smiled. She could almost hear Vasanti's thoughts clearly now.

Amar glanced at the dead dragons around them. "Thanks for your help. I'm glad to see you and Tana have chosen one another, but I sense Haidar is trying to take control of your mind. I don't know how long Tana can hold him back and if Liander joins him, there is no hope of it. We need to get away from here as quickly as possible."

To my lair?

"Yes, I think that would be best. We can perform the Bonding Ceremony for you and Tana unhindered there. But for now I'm afraid I have to do something that will make both of you uncomfortable. To protect your minds from those who would control you."

Amar motioned for Mani to get out the singing stone.

Tana winced. She did not want to hear it or be close to it again, but Mani took it out of the box and tucked it into the pouch on her neck.

The wail of the stone screamed through Tana's mind. She hoped Haidar was close enough to feel the pain as well.

Chapter Nine

Haidar's dragon army made little attempt to stop the Great Green she-dragon from striking out away from the river and deeper into the jungle. Even dragons half mad with hunger would run from a Great Green if they saw it coming. Her body left a trail behind it on the jungle floor, saving Tana the need to use the jungle knife to cut through the underbrush. Mani wore the singing stone. Tana let Mani and Amar follow first behind Vasanti, keeping herself as far back as she could from the stone. If the stone's wail was a song, it was too pain-filled and cruel for anyone to want to hear it. She did not know how Amar could stay so close to his wife while she wore it, but if that's what it took to keep Vasanti's mind free from Haidar's control then Tana would bear it.

Vasanti's wyrmlings clung to her back, two on one side of the sail-like spine and one on the other. They were darling, and to think Amar had been there when they had hatched. Tana would love to have seen it.

After a while Amar fell back to walk with Tana, distancing himself from the stone. His sun-bronzed skin was still too dry, and he was shaking.

"Mani, go on ahead with Vasanti," Tana called. "We need some time away from the stone."

Mani turned back. "I can put it away."

"No don't," Amar said. "It's our best defense. Just keep going with the dragon. She leaves a clear enough trail we won't lose you."

Mani frowned. "All right, but don't get too far behind."

Amar leaned against one of the big trees and waved in agreement.

Tana hacked through a vine that hung down from one of the branches. Clean water ran from its core, and she held it out for the king to drink. He did without arguing, and when it ran dry, Tana cut another for herself to drink and a third to wash the dried dragon and monkey blood from her arms and clothes. Her mind still reeled from the battle. When she'd asked Kanvar to take her hunting with him she'd never imagined in such a short time after she'd have to face an army of dragons as the hunted instead of the hunter.

Amar leaned his head back against the tree trunk and closed his eyes, but his hand rested on his sword hilt.

"Your Majesty, are you angry about Vasanti? Parmver said I could not bond with her because of her poison." Tana shook out her muddy robe, re-rolled it, and tied it onto her back. It seemed silly to give up the obsidian jungle knife she'd worked so hard to make for the robe, but the shimmering gold fabric was like nothing ever made in her village, and the wings she'd worked so hard to sew into it were . . . well, she couldn't help wanting to fly like that again.

Amar chuckled. "Tana, you're brilliant."

Tana realized the singing stone had moved far enough away that she could now feel Amar's mind up close to hers. He'd seen her memory of jumping from the palace window and falling . . . gliding like a Great Green dragon. She struggled to bring her shields back up after the wreck the singing stone had made of her mind. It didn't bother her that Amar had seen her thoughts, but she couldn't risk Haidar finding her again.

"Well . . . it was fun," Tana said. "And the robe is beautiful. I can make another jungle knife."

"You can have mine." Amar rubbed his head and pulled himself upright. "We should keep going."

"Yes, Your Majesty."

Amar took a step and staggered, nearly falling. Tana hurried to his side to help him walk.

"It's all right. I'm fine," he protested, but he let her take his arm to steady him anyway.

They walked on, following the trail of bent grass and broken bushes left in Vasanti's wake. "You didn't answer my question," Tana said after a while.

"You asked a question?" Amar shook his head. "I'm sorry. I'm having a hard time concentrating. I can't think at all when I'm near the singing stone, and when I'm not, it's a constant battle to keep control of my own mind. Forgive me. What was your question?"

Tana used the jungle knife to fling aside a small green snake that hung down in their path. "Parmver said I could not bond with a Great Green dragon, but I want no other than Vasanti. Haidar and Liander, I don't care if they are angry with me, but you . . . I . . . care what you think." Amar's gentle kindness had endeared him to her as much as her own father.

Amar drew in a ragged breath. "It appears the two of you were meant for each other." He was quiet for several more steps before speaking again. "It's ironic, though, since her mate died trying to capture you. He had no right to do it, understand, no right at all, and he was going against my express commands, but he died all the same. I should have realized you were a Naga then when I first went to console Vasanti, but I thought that Mahanth had just been sensing Kanvar."

"You helped her hatch the eggs?" The croak of frogs and buzz of cicadas almost drowned out her question. They'd fallen far enough behind now that even the jungle creatures were returning to song after Vasanti's passing, a much more pleasant song than that of the singing stone.

"She was lonely, and the hutching is an auspicious occasion. Tana, I approve of your bond with Vasanti. You cannot take the place of her mate, but your companionship will do her good."

"And the poison? I'll never be able to touch her except on her dragonstone."

Amar grinned and ran his hand across his chest, brushing condensation off the green dragonscale armor. "I have a solution for that. It will take a bit of alteration, of course, but this armor will look good on you. I made it from the hides of several lesser green dragons. With it, you won't have to keep your distance from Vasanti."

"Your Majesty, you can't. The armor is yours and it is so . . . beautiful."

"Nonesense." Amar patted the hand she had wrapped around his arm to steady his uneven steps. "It's like your jungle knife. I can make more."

The day passed hot and sticky as Amar and Tana trailed behind, talking of the green dragon and her hatchlings, life in the jungle, their favorite foods, anything but what worried each of them most: Rajahansa's betrayal and fall into evil, Parmver's murder, Haidar and Liander's treatment of Tana, and the approaching human army. Tana wanted to question Amar about all of that, but she sensed his constant struggle to keep his mind separate from Rajahansa. His idle chatter was a distraction and a shield against his dragon's demands that he return to the palace.

What bothered Tana the most was Haidar's silence. He made no more attempt to find her mind and sent no more dragons to stop them. She could not believe that he would give up so easily. The silence from Haidar was like the dread when all the jungle animals fall silent in one moment. It could only mean there was something worse to come.

At last, she and Amar reached the hill where Vasanti had delved her lair.

"I've been here before," Tana said, pausing before the low entry.

"Have you? It's a long way from the village," Amar said.

"In my mind, so many times since I lost my mother. I liked to imagine she was still alive, here, in this secret place in my mind. I felt her, though I know now it must have been Vasanti and not my mother at all."

Amar rested his hand against the mossy rock above the opening. "I wonder why, with so many wonderful Great dragons in the world, the Nagas of old limited themselves to bonding only with the Great Gold dragons. It seems strange to me. If only we could go back in time and stop all Khalid's evil from twisting what once was good. We can't do that, of course, but I've spent my whole life trying to right his wrongs, trying to be the kind of king he should have been. I swore when I was young that I would respect all life, that I would force no man or beast against his will, that I would live in peace with humans and Great dragons, that I would do everything in my power to preserve the freedom gained by the world when Stone-fountain fell." Amar choked. His face twisted in sorrow and regret. "Tana . . . Rajahansa wants to release Khalid from Stonefountain and restore the Nagas to power. My own dragon wants to be king of the world, and I see now he'll do anything to accomplish it, kill anyone. . . . His heart is no longer mine. Khalid has twisted it too far. If only we had never sent Devaj to the fountain."

Amar drew in a pained breath. Tana sensed his mind striving with Rajahansa's.

"We should go in," Tana said. "You're weakening. You need the stone to shield you."

"Tana." Amar grabbed her arm in a painful grip. "Khalid cannot be allowed back into this world. Whatever it takes, you must make sure it doesn't happen, even if it means . . . my death. If that is what becomes necessary to stop Rajahansa, I want you to promise me you'll do it."

Fool! Rajahansa's mind broke through Amar's shields and lashed out so loud even Tana could hear it, a twist of punishing pain accompanied it. *You will not stop me. You're death will not bring my own.*

For a moment Tana was caught up in Amar's mind and saw through Rajahansa's eyes, Aadi stripped to the waist, held in Liander's grip while Haidar slathered his skin with a sickening yellow ointment.

"No, please, it burns," Aadi cried.

"It's necessary to bring on the fever," Haidar said. "Don't you want to bond with Rajahansa, Aadi? Don't you want to be king?"

"No. Amar is the king." Aadi tried to pull away, but Haidar sliced into Aadi's mind and took control of his body. The boy stood there shaking as Haidar finished covering him with the ointment.

"Amar is king no longer. He has abandoned his throne, and you, Aadi, will replace him," Haidar said while he worked Aadi over.

"But Amar is still bound to Rajahansa, he can't bond with two Nagas at the same time, can he?"

Haidar laughed. "Khalid says this will work. It has been done before, secretly in the past. A combination of the ointment and your skin in direct contact with Rajahansa's will force the fever on you early. You will bond with Rajahansa, become his second Naga, and fly with him to Stonefountain."

"No, please." Aadi cringed as Rajahansa lifted Aadi out of Liander's grip and coiled his body around the boy, rubbing golden plates against Aadi's exposed skin.

No! Amar screamed. *Stop. This is the height of all perversion to force the fever and a bond on an innocent child, to pollute your bond with me by bonding with another as well. You cannot stoop to this level of filth.*

Rajahansa laughed and licked Aadi's face. *I don't need you anymore, Amar. You can stay in the jungle and rot forever. Khalid and I will rule this world.*

Tana's stomach churned. She tried to pull her mind free, but it was too wound up in the battle as Amar used all his power and might to try and take control of Rajahansa and stop him. To no avail.

Amar stopped struggling and spoke in a mental whisper. *All right, Raj, you win. I propose a trade. You can't be sure what you're doing to Aadi will not kill him. Take me instead. Bring Aadi here and set him free, and I will submit myself to your command. No more fighting, no more trying to escape. Whatever you want. Just let Aadi go.*

Chapter Ten

Tana's mind untangled from Amar's, and she felt tears coursing down her cheeks.

Amar gasped, blinked, and looked at her. "You saw?"

Tana nodded.

"I have no choice. I can't let him hurt Aadi like this. Tana . . . you have to understand."

"I understand, Your Majesty." Tana felt sick beyond the fever that burned inside her, sick like the sludge of a human waste heap.

"What I told you before he broke through my shields, I mean it. You must tell Kanvar everything. Make sure he understands. Here—" Amar unbuckled the sword from his waist and held it out to Tana. "You need this to bond. Give it to Kanvar afterward. Tell Mani I'm sorry. I love her."

Tana took the sword gingerly, holding onto the sheath and avoiding the hilt. "You should tell her yourself."

"No time." Amar stripped his armor off and laid it at Tana's feet with the rest of his gear then started up the hillside. Trees grew up the slope, but a gray precipice rose above that. "I'll send Aadi down to you. Get the ointment washed off him quickly. With any luck he won't have had contact with Rajahansa for long enough to force the fever. Tell Mani she must be a mother to him. To care for him as if he were her own son. It will ease the sting for her if she has someone to look after."

"Majesty" Tana started up after him.

"No, stay." He waved her back down. "Stay beneath the trees where it's safe, and make sure Mani stays as well. Whatever else, don't let her come up here. I need to know she's safe. If my life and soul must be forfeit, I must know that the rest of you are free from Rajahansa's clutches."

Tana's heart beat in sick regret as she watched Amar disappear up the slope. The horror of what she'd seen and knew bound her lungs so she could hardly draw a breath. She was still frozen in place, gazing up the slope, when Mani ducked out of the lair several minutes later. She carried the singing stone in its box in one hand and had Amar's crossbow strapped on her back.

"There you are," Mani said. "I was starting to worry. Where's Amar?"

Tana shook her head. Her throat was too tight to speak.

Mani looked around. Her face paled with fear as she realized Amar wasn't with Tana but his armor and sword were. She grabbed Tana's arm. "Tana, what happened? Where is he?"

Tana swallowed and forced the thick words from her mouth. "Rajahansa threatened to . . ." what words could she use to describe the perversion Rajahansa had planned for Aadi? " . . . hurt Aadi if Amar did not return to the palace. He's gone." Tana pointed up the hill. "Up above the canopy to meet Rajahansa."

"No." Mani hiked her dress and scrambled up the hill.

Tana raced after her, catching her arm, and dragging her to a stop. "You can't go up there, Mani. He's giving his life to keep the rest of us safe. Don't throw that away."

"You let him go? How could you let him go? Do you have any idea what Rajahansa plans to do to him?" Mani tore free and started up the hill once more.

Tana sprinted after her and tackled her, forcing her to the ground amid the damp ferns. The smell of fungus and decaying leaves flung up around them as they wrestled on the slope. Overhead, wings flapped and a gold dragon trumpeted.

"Let me go," Mani yelled, tearing at Tana's hair and trying to throw her off.

"I can't." Tana struggled to keep the queen pinned to the ground. "I promised him I'd keep you safe. Your Majesty, Amar wants you to be free. You need to take care of Aadi. He's hurt, and he needs you."

Mani clawed at Tana's face, broke loose, and freed the singing stone from the iron box. "Whatever he told you isn't true. Rajahansa has control of his mind. I have to free him. Do not try to stop me again, or I will kill you."

Tana scrambled to her feet and shook her head. The motion did nothing to lessen the wail of the singing stone. "Mani, please."

"No. Stay back." Mani slipped the singing stone into place in the pouch on her neck and drew the crossbow.

Tana tried to grab her before she could get it loaded, but Mani hit her with it and raced toward the sound of the dragon on the rocks above the trees. Tana followed. By the time she got in reach again, Mani had the weapon loaded.

Tana froze with the loaded crossbow only an arm's length from her face. "Mani, don't do anything crazy."

"I'm not being crazy. You are." Mani's finger rested just above the trigger. "Now, I'm going up there and you will not try to stop me."

"All right. I'll wait here. You get Aadi and bring him down. He'll need a bath as soon as we get our hands on him. I saw a stream down there close to the lair. We need to get him into it."

"I'll bring them both back."

Tana let her go ahead and then followed up the hill to the cliffs that jutted above the trees. A field of weathered rock fallen from the face of the precipice had accumulated at the base. Mani scrambled up the rocks, climbing above the canopy. Tana stayed down beneath the trees. With the wail of the singing stone slashing her mind, she couldn't tell if Haidar and Liander had accompanied Rajahansa or not. She couldn't risk being captured, not when the king had laid such a terrible task on her.

Through the thick branches, she heard Rajahansa's angry roar as the singing stone came within his range.

"Amar!" Mani shouted. "Come back."

"Mani, I love you. I can't. Look after Aadi," Amar responded. Heavy dragon wings beat the air and faded away.

Tana sank to her knees. Her heart felt stripped of emotion, the air too heavy to pull into her lungs. Chills shook her body. The itch on her chest spread to her arms, and when she scratched it, flakes of scaly white skin came away beneath her fingernails. An overwhelming emptiness swept over her. She knelt there for . . . she didn't know how long until Aadi's voice made her look up.

"Tana." Aadi scrambled off the rock-fall and raced toward her. Bloody red lesions marred his chest and arms where Haidar had spread the ointment. His black hair was a tangled mess. Aadi was younger than Tana, but his lean body stood an inch taller than her as he caught her up in a relieved hug. "I-I thought you were dead. You jumped and . . . it's so far down."

Tana had known Aadi in the village before he went to the palace, and she'd spent some time with him when she had arrived in the golden halls. They'd been casual friends, but Aadi seemed happy to see her even after all he'd been through.

"Where's the queen?" Tana asked him.

Aadi shook his head. "She's up there on the rocks, crying. I couldn't get her to come down." He smelled like the pungent ointment, and Tana's skin burned from it where her bare hand came in contact with his arm.

Tana hesitated, torn between looking after the queen and helping Aadi.

"Do you want me to go back up and carry her down?" Aadi asked.

"No, Aadi. You're hurt. His Majesty said we have to get that ointment washed off you immediately. There's a stream down at the base of this hill. Go wash off, right now, quickly." Tana nudged him down the slope.

He took two steps and stopped, staring at a trail of gouges going up one of the large gray tree trunks. "Tana, those are . . . Great Green dragon claw marks. They have to be. No other dragon claws below the canopy are as big. And this hill, it's just the type of place—"

"Her name's Vasanti, and she's a friend. Trust me, she won't hurt you."

"She may have wyrmlings and—"

"She has three. Just go and wash in the stream, Aadi. I'll be right down." Tana headed for the rocks, but the hair on the back of her neck prickled in fear of finding Haidar waiting for her just above the trees. With the singing stone blocking her mind and the sunlight that would hide his dragon, she wouldn't see him until it was too late. But she couldn't leave the queen up there exposed.

Aadi screamed.

Tana turned back and saw Vasanti lunging up the slope, claws flashing, teeth bared. She swept past Aadi and bounded up the rocks. The singing stone blocked the dragon's intentions from Tana, but she had no fear that Vasanti would hurt her. The rock-fall was an easy climb for the green dragon that could scale vertical surfaces and hang upside down on tree limbs.

From beneath the trees, Tana heard a gold dragon yelp, and a man cry out in fear. Vasanti roared and her claws scraped against the cliff face. The gold dragon took to the air, wings flapping hard.

"Tana!" Haidar yelled down through the canopy. "I will get my hands on you. I promise you that. Someday I'll—"

Another roar from Vasanti drowned out his voice.

A moment later Vasanti slithered down off the rock-slide, carrying a paralyzed Mani like prey in her tail.

"No." Aadi lunged at the green dragon as Vasanti tried to pass him on the way back down, but Tana reached Aadi first, blocking him.

"Aadi, she's fine. The poison wears off in a few hours. She'll be all right. Come on. It's you we need to take care of." Tana kept her grip on Aadi's arm as she led him back down to the base of the hill.

"She won't be fine when the dragon eats her," Aadi said.

"Vasanti won't eat Mani."

"How can you be sure?" Aadi stopped beside the knee-high stream that ran down beyond the lair.

Tana let out a sheepish laugh. "She's my dragon, Aadi. I'm going to bond with her. King Amar said I could, that I should, that we'd be good for each other."

"The king told you to bond with a green dragon? I don't believe it."

"Believe it, Aadi." Tana hooked her foot behind Aadi's legs and shoved him in the chest. He splashed backward into the stream. She jumped in after him, snatching up soft moss to scrub the ointment from his chest and arms.

"Ouch," Aadi complained, trying to push her away. "That hurts. Leave me alone."

"The king also told me to wash this filth off you. You'll get the fever when it's time to get the fever and not before. I hope."

Aadi stopped fighting and let Tana finish cleaning the ointment from his body. When they both climbed out of the water, the lesions on his skin seeped with blood. Aadi shuddered and swiped his wet hair out of his eyes.

"I'm sorry they did this to you," Tana said. "It's like they've gone crazy."

Aadi grimaced. "I've got to get back to the palace, Tana. Do you think the green dragon will help me? She can climb the cliff to get up there, can't she?"

"I'm sure she can, but why go back after they did this to you?"

Aadi glanced down at the painful sores that spread across his body. "They have Parmver locked up somewhere. They won't tell me where. They said he'd gone to stay at the village, but I don't believe them. All his things are still in his room: his clothes, his tools, his books, his medicines. Parmver is . . . you haven't known him for as long as I have, Tana. He's like . . . everything to me. I have to go back and save him."

Tana shivered. Her chills settled down into her bones. Her eyes stung. She had to speak, but she didn't want to do it.

"Tana, please. Tell your dragon to take me back there."

Tana splashed away from the water and retrieved the jungle knife and Amar's sword and armor. "We have a Bonding Ceremony to perform first." She knew she should tell Aadi about Parmver's murder. She promised herself she would . . . soon.

The smell of moss and jungle flowers met her as she ducked through the low entrance of Vasanti's lair. Inside was the beautiful main chamber decorated with Vasanti's colorful moss murals. In the center of the room, Vasanti's three wyrmlings wrestled with each other in the nest. Vasanti's tail snaked out from an adjoining chamber.

Mani's singing stone went silent.

Tana sighed in relief and rubbed her head as she crossed the chamber. Avoiding contact with Vasanti, she slid into the other chamber where the dragon had taken Mani. It was a large moss-covered room with slits in the wall that let in light from outside. Woven shelves lined part of the curved wall, holding up baskets of herbs and dried flowers, beautifully matched wooden bowls carved with jungle scenes, and ceramic pots fashioned to look like jungle animals. Vasanti's handiwork surpassed even that of the most skilled villagers.

I'm older than anyone in your village, Vasanti said, tucking the paralyzed Mani down into a mossy chair. *Human life spans are so short.*

"Is she going to be all right?" Tana asked.

Mani's eyes were opened and tears still leaked from them, but her body lay limp against the chair where Vasanti had set her.

She'll recover from the poison soon, Vasanti said. *But her broken heart won't be so easy to heal. She loved him, I think, and fears she will never see him again.*

Tana smiled bitterly. Her communication with Vasanti was still something a little less than clear speech, but they understood each other well enough, and Vasanti could see the images in Tana's head that Amar's mind had left there.

She has reason to fear then. Vasanti filled a wooden cup with water from one of the pots and lifted it to Mani's mouth so she could drink.

Aadi pushed past Tana into the room and went to the queen. Vasanti drew back so he wouldn't rub against her poisoned scales. *His wounds look painful*, she thought to Tana. *Tell him to hold still.* Vasanti set down the cup.

"Aadi." Tana moved over beside him and took hold of his arm. "You know Great dragon saliva can heal wounds."

"Yes. Parmver always kept some with him."

"Good. Hold still."

Aadi yelped as Vasanti's long tongue snaked out and licked him, slathering the saliva across his chest and arms.

"Turn." Tana twisted him around so Vasanti could lick his back as well.

"I can't believe I'm in a Great Green dragon lair," Aadi said. "I just can't believe it." He turned back to face Vasanti. "Oh, Mighty Great dragon, will you please return me to the palace. There is someone still there we have to save."

Tana sighed and dumped the remaining water from the cup back into the ceramic pot. "Parmver's dead."

"What? No he's not."

"Yes, Aadi. I was there. After the king escaped, Rajahansa blamed Parmver and murdered him. He killed him, Aadi. Parmver's gone."

Aadi stared at her, his face blank as if her words had flown past his head like down from a seedpod.

Tana untied the golden robe from her back and slipped it on over her clothes. "Aadi, look at me. I can't breathe. The rash has spread all the way down my arms. If I don't bond now, I'm going to die too. The king was going to help me, but he's gone. I need you. Mani and I both need you. Don't go back to the palace. Parmver isn't there."

Aadi blinked.

Tana went back to the central chamber to retrieve the king's sword.

Vasanti settled onto her nest, and her wyrmlings curled up beside her.

"They're beautiful," Tana said, watching the little creatures nestle with their mother.

As are you.

Tana's face grew warm. She twisted the cup in her hand. "Do you know anything about the Bonding Ceremony?"

Only what I see in your mind, Vasanti said.

"I'm frightened. I don't want to cut myself. And . . . I don't know if I can actually drink the . . . blood."

I imagine your blood will be very sweet. Vasanti chuckled and licked Tana's face.

Tana winced, and her stomach rebelled at the thought of what she must do. The fever made her dizzy, and her chest hurt with each breath she took. "I think I'm dying." She sank to the floor, the sheathed sword in one hand and cup in the other.

Aadi stepped into the central chamber, his face bleak, his fists clenched. "There is a right way to do this ceremony, and this is not it. The king must officiate. And you *have* to bond to a gold dragon."

"The king gave me his blessing for this. If you're not going to help, get out and leave me alone." Tana dumped the sword from its sheath onto the ground so she could reach her wrist to the tip of the blade without having to hold the hilt.

"Kanvar broke the rules and look what happened; he's destroyed everything we love." Aadi kicked the sword away from Tana.

Tana jumped to her feet. "Kanvar didn't do any of this. Rajahansa did. He's allied himself with Khalid, and that evil is what split the Nagas in the palace. That evil is what killed Parmver. Rajahansa hurt you. He desecrated your flesh and planned to feed you body and soul to Khalid. How can you even think to side with him?"

Aadi grabbed Tana's wrist. "I'm not siding with him. I just . . . Parmver taught me the way things are supposed to be done is all. I don't want to believe that Parmver is dead, but if he is, someone has to carry on the things he taught. Haidar and Liander have rejected all the things he believed in. That only leaves you and me."

"And Kanvar, Devaj, Karishi, and Denali." Tana eased her wrist out of Aadi's grip.

Aadi grimaced. "Devaj has abandoned us, Denali is too young, Karishi has gone into hiding in the mountain by the village, and Kanvar . . . Kanvar is an arrogant, rash, selfish, pile of dragon droppings. You plan to bond with this Great Green dragon? You do realize this may be the mate of the dragon Kanvar murdered?"

Vasanti rose to her feet, hissing.

Aadi tensed and stepped away from Tana.

"I suppose Parmver told you that as well," Tana said.

"Yes, of course he did."

Tana clenched the wooden cup in her hand. "I don't care what you think of Kanvar. I am going to bond with Vasanti."

"Not if I can help it." Aadi gripped her shoulders. "Tana, there are plenty of gold dragons to bond with."

Tana tried to pull away. But she was too dizzy. She could no longer fight off the dragon sickness. *Kanvar*, she cried out with the last of her strength. *Kanvar, help me!* Then blackness sucked her into its arms.

Chapter Eleven

Kanvar stared out across the rolling waves at the approaching fleet of ships. Both Varnan and Maran flags flapped from the masts. The two countries that had so often battled one another had joined for a single cause, to put down the Naga threat.

Beneath Kanvar, Dharanidhar growled and shifted on his perch atop the cliffs overlooking the ocean. Having located a new place for the Great Blue dragon pride to live, Dharanidhar and Kanvar had flown to the opposite coast in search of Tana and Kanvar's parents who, it seemed, had escaped from the palace. Their search had brought them into the face of the approaching army.

Too many humans to stop, Dharanidhar said.

Frost, who clung to Dharanidhar's back behind Kanvar, burbled in agreement. She'd stuck with Dhar and

Kanvar ever since the blue dragons had gone to the new nesting grounds.

"Haidar will fight them anyway," Kanvar said. "He's taken control of just about anything with teeth and claws that moves in the jungle. A lot of people, both dragons and men, will die." Kanvar's hand curled into a fist. "I suppose it is my fault like Jabari said. I tried to help the humans. I went to their aid, and this is what we get because of it. I should have listened to Rajahansa. For once I should have just listened."

Rajahansa is a fool, Kanvar. Like you told Jabari, you didn't start this. Kumar Raza's brother did.

"Rajan had no control over himself. It was Erebus the Devourer, the Great Red dragon, who kicked the ant hill."

Then we should not be surprised that the fire ants have swarmed out. Dharanidhar breathed a spurt of blue fire.

"Those ships carry more than ants. Those are soldiers and dragon hunters. Thousands of them. Your old enemy has returned. Too many to fight this time." Kanvar reached over his shoulder to stroke his crossbow.

Behind Kanvar, Frost's dragonstone flashed as if she could blind the entire fleet even that far away. *Stupid humans. They'll never find our new nesting grounds.*

Kanvar chuckled. He was relieved that the blue dragons had completed their move to new caves on the western coast. *Devaj, are all the villagers out now?* Kanvar called to his brother.

Ah, Kanvar. Waves of exhaustion emanated through the mental connection. *Yes, Elkatran, I, and Bensharie are carrying the last to the new village now.*

Thank you, Devaj. Dhar and I will meet you there, just as soon as we locate Tana and our parents and pick them up. Kanvar rubbed Dharanidhar's neck. "I guess we've rested long enough."

Right then, let's go find your parents, Dharanidhar rumbled and took to the air. His flight was slow and deliberate. He glided on the rising hot air currents as much as he could, sparing his wings and using the least amount of energy possible for flight. Kanvar was just glad to have him in the air again.

I'm worried about Tana, he thought to Dharanidhar. Kanvar hadn't heard anything from her since she said she and Kanvar's parents were out of the palace. Haidar had been trying to take control of her mind, and Kanvar fought him so she could break free. Both he and Haidar had lost track of her then.

She's got to be down in the jungle somewhere. We just need to keep looking.

They had been looking for some time already, skimming across the tops of the trees and feeling for her presence. But the last place Kanvar had felt her was too close to the palace for Dharanidhar to fly safely. The gold dragons were on constant watch for the blues.

Kanvar, help me! Tana's cry came to him faintly from the densest part of the jungle, but cut off as suddenly as it sounded.

"Dhar," Kanvar shouted, urging Dharanidhar to change direction and speed his flight toward where the cry had come from. *I can't feel her mind, Dhar. It was there and then gone so fast.*

We got the general direction anyway. Dharanidhar pressed himself to fly at full speed and was soon circling a gray precipice of rock surrounded at the base by dense trees.

Tana, Kanvar searched below with his mind, looking for any flicker of human thought. He was surprised to find Mani and Aadi in paralyzed shock inside a Great Green dragon lair. He could see the dragon through Aadi's mind, standing over Tana who lay unconscious on the mossy floor of the lair.

Dhar let out a roar and swooped down to land on a rockslide that skirted the cliff just above the tree tops. Kanvar unbuckled himself and Dharanidhar lifted him down to the ground. The rocks wobbled beneath him, and he nearly fell.

Dharanidhar caught him. *How are you going to get down this?*

"I'll slide on my butt if I have to," Kanvar said, inching down the rocks.

Frost let out a chirp and swooped down the slope into the trees. She was small enough the dense growth did not stop her, though the heat repelled her. *Be careful*, Kanvar called. *Just distract the dragon from Tana. Don't get her angry. I don't want you hurt.*

While Kanvar eased himself down the rocky slope, fretting about his slow progress, he followed Frost's mind as she reached the base of the hill and fluttered into the green dragon's lair.

Hey, Frost said to the ferocious green she-dragon. *Leave my Tana alone.*

The she-dragon turned to face Frost. *What . . . are you? Little one, wyrmling. You have no color.*

Frost flashed her dragonstone in the green dragon's face, filling the dim lair with a blinding white light.

The green dragon howled in surprise and turned her head away.

Frost flapped over to Tana and stood guard over her. *My Tana, not yours. You no hurt her.*

Blind me, you little scamp? The green dragon picked up Frost with her teeth by the scruff of her neck and carried her to a nest in the center of the chamber. *I suppose you're lost and hungry. Wait here with the others, I'll bring dinner soon.* She put Frost down into the nest with three green dragon wyrmlings who cooed and rubbed up against Frost. Fortunately, the wyrmlings were too young to produce the paralyzing poison of adult Great Green dragons.

Frost hissed and spread her wings. *We do not eat humans.*

No, of course not, little one. The she-dragon rubbed her eyes.

You have three trapped in your lair.

Kanvar twisted his good leg on a loose rock and tumbled forward. Rocks and gravel gave way beneath the impact of his body, and he slid on his chest the rest of the way down the slope. He groaned when he came to a stop at the base of the loose rocks. At least the sharp rocks had torn gouges in his armor and not his flesh. But in the fall, he'd missed part of Frost's conversation with the dragon. He dragged himself upright and started down the mossy hill.

Aadi hurt Tana? Frost said. The little white dragon was confused, and Kanvar was confused along with her.

Aadi did not want Tana and I to bond, the green dragon said. *He thinks she should bond with a gold dragon, but Tana and I have already chosen each other.*

Kanvar remembered then that Tana had said she wanted to bond with a Great Green dragon. Of course she would be at this dragon's lair. Scrapped, bruised, and breathing hard, Kanvar made it to the base of the hill. A low entrance led underground. Taking a deep breath, Kanvar ducked inside. His instinct was to draw his crossbow first, but if Tana had chosen the Great Green she-dragon to bond with, Kanvar figured it might be friendly to him.

What Kanvar saw from just inside the entrance took his breath away. The lair was nothing like a muddy hole in the ground; it was more a work of art, fashioned over hundreds of years.

Frost burbled happily from the nest in the center where she'd started to play with the green wyrmlings. The Great Green she-dragon turned toward Kanvar, still trying to blink the light from her eyes so she could see.

"My name is Kanvar." Kanvar bowed just in case the dragon could sort-of see him. "May I enter your home?"

An angry rumble welled up in the dragon's throat.

"I believe Tana is hurt. She needs me. She called for my help."

I know she called you, the dragon said. *She's fallen unconscious and I fear she might die, but you—* The dragon's tail lashed petulantly across the back of the chamber. *—should know I don't think I can ever forgive you for murdering my husband. I'll tolerate you for Tana's sake. But what you have done cannot be undone. I am alone, and my children grow up without a father.*

Kanvar's breath caught in his throat. He'd only killed one Great Green dragon. "He-he was attacking Tana."

I know what he was doing. And I know you did not understand. He sensed Tana was a Naga, and he wanted to catch her and take her to the king for a reward. He was foolish, always so terribly foolish, and he died for it. But he never meant to hurt her. The green dragon lowered her head and moaned.

Kanvar lifted his hand toward the dragon. "I am sorry. So, so sorry."

The green dragon heaved a heavy sigh. *The queen and the village boy are in the side chamber to your right. They are paralyzed but unhurt. My name is Vasanti. You may enter my lair. You must wake Tana and help her bond with me. She is frightened of the cut and the blood. Aadi would not help her and tried to run away when she fell unconscious. I paralyzed him because I don't think he would survive for long alone in the jungle.*

"Where's my father?" Kanvar limped across the mossy floor and knelt next to Tana. Her breathing was labored, her face waxy.

Vasanti groaned and sunk to the ground, keeping her tail and torso away from the Kanvar and Tana. *The king gave himself up to Rajahansa in trade for Aadi's freedom.*

"What?" Kanvar gathered his father's sword and a wooden cup he found on the ground beside Tana.

He's gone back to the palace. The other Nagas were working some fell craft on Aadi to force him to bond with Rajahansa.

Kanvar caught a flash picture from Vasanti's mind of images Tana had seen of happenings in the palace. Kanvar caught his breath. "Can he do that? Could he really bond with more than one Naga?"

I don't know. Vasanti said. *It seems the king was convinced of the possibility.*

"But Parmver would never let them do such a thing."

The Naga you call Parmver is dead. I have seen it in Tana's mind.

"Oh no." Kanvar could not hold back the sorrow that washed over him. He'd allowed himself some hope when Tana had said his father was free, but that hope seeped away as he grappled with the implications of what Vasanti had told him.

Blue Naga. We do not have time for your worry and grief. Wake Tana now, before we lose her, Vansanti said.

Kanvar bit back his sorrow. Sitting, he pulled Tana's head and torso onto his lap and cradled her head in his arm. "Tana," he whispered, finding his way into her darkened mind. "Tana, wake up." She had swooned, but her mind was not locked away as Kumar Raza's had been when Kanvar had entered that blackness.

Kanvar? Tana moaned and opened her eyes. She blinked and then clutched his arm. "Kanvar, help me." She looked around. "Where is Aadi? He . . . tried to keep me from bonding, but your father told me I could. He said it was all right. You have to believe me."

"I believe you." Kanvar brushed a stray hair out of Tana's face. "I'm sure my father would approve of this bond. Aadi just thinks everything should be done properly. He's safe. Vasanti paralyzed him."

Tana let out a sigh of relief.

Kanvar smiled down at her, trying to look reassuring. "Vasanti tells me you are frightened of this ceremony."

Tana nodded. "I . . . the cut. I can't do it."

"Don't worry. Just look away. You won't feel a thing. I promise."

"How?"

"Trust me. You have to let me into your mind and trust me." Kanvar brushed his thoughts up against Tana's shields. She held them against him for a moment, then hesitantly let them down.

Kanvar took a deep breath. He'd never blocked a person's sense of pain before, only felt his father do it to him when he cleaned the infected sword wound in his leg. He did not want to hurt Tana's mind or invade any thoughts she deemed private. He pulled up the sleeve of her robe, brushed his fingers down her arm, and let them rest against her wrist. "Can you focus for a moment on the touch of my hand, please? Don't think of anything else, just the spot where I'm touching you."

Tana pulled her wrist away from him. "N-no, it's going to hurt. Don't cut me. Not yet. I'm not ready."

"I don't even have the sword in my hand. How can I cut you? I promise I won't do it as long as you can feel my fingers against your wrist." He lifted her hand back onto his lap and repositioned his fingers against her wrist. Her vein throbbed beneath the pressure of his touch. "You can feel my hand?"

"Yes."

"Good, now think about only that so I can follow your thoughts. I'm going to enter your mind now. You can tell me to stop if it is uncomfortable." Kanvar let his thoughts slip into Tana's mind. She tensed but did not order him to stop. Her thoughts were a swirl of fear and sorrow, but they were tame compared to the seething mess Rajan's mind had been after they had freed him from the red dragon. Ignoring everything else in her mind, Kanvar found her sense of feeling and focused on it. Nothing existed except the pressure of his fingers against her wrist. Then he twisted her thoughts just a little, the barest trickle of compulsion not to feel her arm.

Tana gasped. "My arm, I can't—"

"It's all right. You'll feel it again in a moment." Kanvar gently turned Tana's head so she could not see her arm, lifted the sword, and pressed the tip against her wrist. "Can you feel that?"

"I can't feel anything. I'm frightened."

"Don't be." Kanvar nicked her wrist with the sword then set it aside and lifted the cup into place to catch the blood. *Vasanti, lick the wound closed*, Kanvar told the dragon as soon as the cup held what he figured was enough blood.

Vasanti stretched her head close while keeping the rest of her body well back and licked the cut. The skin healed over, leaving a one inch scar on Tana's wrist.

Kanvar smiled and withdrew his influence from Tana's mind. "There, see. Nothing to be frightened of."

Tana stirred in his lap, and lifted her arm up where she could see it. She let out a little laugh. "That was . . . all right, I guess."

"Good. Well, on to the next bit then. I'm glad I have armor so I won't be paralyzed touching Vasanti. Can you sit, Tana?"

Tana drew herself off him and sat, but she was shaking, and he feared she might swoon again if he did not hurry.

"Vasanti, are you ready?"

The dragon held out her foreleg. *Of course. I fear no human blade.*

Kanvar cut her, and the blood flowed into the cup. When it was ready, Kanvar held it out for Tana to drink.

Chapter Twelve

Tana took the cup from Kanvar, but her hand shook so much she almost dropped it.

"Here." Kanvar wrapped his own hand around hers to steady the cup and slid close to support her back against his chest.

Tana shivered. Though his presence beside her gave her strength and courage, the chills from the fever wracked her body. "I'm glad you're here," she whispered.

Despite the way Haidar had tried to manipulate her mind to hate Kanvar, she felt better being near him. She had sensed genuine affection and care for her wellbeing from Kanvar. As she felt him again now, she realized it was that *sense* of person that made the difference between him and Haidar. Haidar was all greed and lust while Kanvar was gentle companionship, with a subtle underflow of surprise that she would allow him to touch her rather than shy away from his deformity.

"I'm glad I found you. Now drink. You'll only get sicker until you do." He lifted the cup to her lips.

The polished wood was smooth against her mouth, but the smell of the blood made her gag. "Kanvar, I can't."

"I thought you *wanted* to bond with Vasanti?"

"I do. But this is too hard, too much to ask." Tana twisted her head away from the cup.

"Just plug your nose and pretend it's one of Parmver's medicines. Those taste vile enough. Come on. You don't have to drink it all. Just a couple of swallows." Kanvar brushed her cheek with his stumpy left hand.

She shuddered. "It's too gross."

"It's better than dying."

Tana took a shaky breath and turned her head back to the cup. She parted her lips and pressed them against the rim. Kanvar lifted the cup, and the viscous liquid poured into her mouth, spreading across her tongue, tasting of salt and sweat and raw meat. She gagged and coughed. Her stomach heaved, but she clamped her mouth shut, tipped her head back, and swallowed. Then she opened her mouth and gasped.

"One more sip," Kanvar whispered, moving the cup back to her lips. "Just to make sure it's enough."

She relented. The taste already clung to her tongue and, no matter how she swallowed, wouldn't wash away.

She drank two more swallows then pulled away from Kanvar and lay down on the moss. She was so dizzy and her stomach twisted in revulsion.

"I'll get you some water." Kanvar handed the cup to Vasanti who lapped up the rest of the blood.

There's water in the chamber to the right. Vasanti's words sounded crisp and clear in Tana's mind.

Tana tried to laugh in joy at hearing Vasanti talk, but the laugh came out more of a moan. Heat tingled through her body, starting from her chest and spreading outward. Her chills faded, replaced by tremors. She tried to stop shaking but couldn't.

Kanvar returned to her side. "It's a beautiful robe," he said, smoothing the shimmering fabric.

"It's more than just beautiful," Tana said through the taste of blood that still clung to her mouth. "It's my wings." She shared with Kanvar her memory of jumping from the palace windows and falling, falling, and then spreading her arms and legs to glide above the tress.

"That's amazing," Kanvar said in awe. "Makes me want to try it myself. So very much like how a green dragon jumps from tree to tree."

"That's where I got the idea."

"Here." Kanvar helped her sit and gave her the water. She swirled it around in her mouth and spit it out several times before drinking the rest. Her tremors subsided and a feeling of peace and wholeness spread over her. Joy swelled her heart.

"Vasanti." She reached out to hug her dragon in supreme gratitude to become one with such a wondrous creature.

Vasanti shook her head and backed away. *Not yet, my beautiful friend.* She hooked the king's green armor with her foreclaw and laid it down beside Tana. *Adjust the armor and put it on while I go hunting. The children are hungry. It's been far too long since they last ate. I will leave them in your care and be back shortly. Then, you and I shall have a proper greeting.*

Tana watched Vasanti slither out of the lair. Part of her went with the dragon and part of her stayed nestled against Kanvar's chest.

"Better now?" Kanvar said. "You see, not so bad. Everything is all right."

Tana swallowed. Part of her felt happier than she'd ever been in her life, but she knew that everything was not all right. She hated to ruin this moment with Kanvar, but the king's command compelled her to speak.

"Nothing's all right," she said. "I have a message for you from your father. He gave himself up to free Aadi. Rajahansa intends to take Amar to Stonefountain and give his body to Khalid. Your father—mind, body, and soul—will be controlled by the evil tyrant. He bade me give you the sword and tell you that you must not let this happen. Whatever it takes, whatever you have to do, you can't let Rajahansa fly him to Stonefountain."

Kanvar stiffened.

"I'm sorry, Kanvar. Your father did it for Aadi. Rajahansa would have taken him to Khalid instead if your father had not intervened." Tana's breathing became easier as the fever cooled and the tightness in her chest faded.

Kanvar brushed at his eyes and stood up. "I can't believer Rajahansa would hurt Aadi like that."

"He killed Parmver. Don't you understand? He'll stop at nothing to gain Khalid's power. Khalid has him convinced that together they can restore the ancient civilization and might of Stonefountain."

Kanvar's face flushed and he snatched up the sword. "Rajahansa . . . killed . . . Parmver? Vasanti said Parmver was dead, but not that Rajahansa had murdered him. Why would he do that?"

"For helping the king escape the palace," Tana said.

"By the fires of all the volcanoes, how could such evil come back into our world?" Kanvar said. Overhead, a Great Blue dragon roar split the sky. "We will stop this, Tana. The blue dragons and I will not let the slavery and abuses of Stonefountain return. I will not let my father be destroyed by Khalid. I came here to get you and my parents and take you all to safety. But I can't do that now. I have to warn the other blue dragons that my father is no longer free." Kanvar limped out of the lair.

Tana watched him go, running off again after only spending a few minutes with her. Would it always be like that? She took a step to follow him. "Kanvar, wait, I can help you."

Kanvar ducked back into the lair and glanced over at the wyrmlings. They crawled up to the lip of the nest and blinked at him with big green eyes. Frost had joined them, looking strangely pale beside the green dragons. "I'll take you willingly, Tana, but will the children be safe if you leave them? What about Mani and Aadi. Who will look after them in the jungle?"

"I think we should take them too. They won't be happy here, but I don't know where we could take them. The village won't be safe."

Kanvar rubbed his hand along the sword hilt. "No, the village isn't safe. The human armies have arrived. Devaj has moved all your friends and family to a safe spot. I'll call him to come get Aadi and Mani and take them to safety with the others. Frost, I want you to go with Devaj."

Frost burbled a complaint, but agreed to do as Kanvar said.

Tana picked up the king's good steel jungle knife from where she'd dropped it when she entered the lair. Kanvar's blue dragon roared again, shaking the trees outside. She looked from Kanvar to the wyrmlings and back to Kanvar. "I . . . she's trusting me to keep them safe."

"I know." Kanvar limped over to her. "Stay here and keep them safe. You can help me later. I imagine we'll have to guard the coast to keep Rajahansa in Kundiland for quite some time. Call me when you're free to join me. I'll come for you." He kissed her on the forehead and hurried back out of the cave.

This time she let him go. Her mind swirled in disbelief. She'd given Kanvar the king's message, but he hadn't understood it. If his only intention was to keep Rajahansa and Amar in Kundiland, he had not interpreted things correctly. No matter how hard he tried, sooner or later, Rajahansa would sneak or fight his way past the blue dragons.

"He can't do it," she muttered. "He loves his father too much." Tana loved Amar too. No man's presence was as dear as the king's. When Tana looked into his face, she knew he loved and valued her beyond what she even valued herself. Amar was gentle and kind, soft spoken and patient, a father to all, the kind of king any man would wish to serve because Amar's sole purpose was to give his own life in service to others.

That's why I have to kill him, Tana told herself. If Kanvar can't do it, I must carry out the king's commands. His only freedom from Rajahansa's evil is in death. Fingering the jungle knife, she paced around the chamber. The wyrmlings watched her, their curious thoughts rubbing up against Tana's mind. Was she food? Would she feed them? Did she know where food was? When would their mother return with food?

Tana laughed. If only feeding the babies was all she had to worry about. She and Vasanti would have to return to the palace tonight. Vasanti could carry Tana in her tail up the cliff and in through the windows. She'd need the armor for that, of course. She went to Amar's armor and looked it over to see what modifications were necessary. Shortening the legs and the sleeves. Letting out a bit in the chest and tucking the shoulders and waist in. She could do it easily with the right tools.

Vasanti? she asked.

Vasanti's mind was focused on catching a fat black monkey. *Sh, Tana, I'm hunting.*

Do you have any tools for working leather?

Yes, in a basket on the shelves. The monkey climbed past the branch where Vasanti waited. She moved her tail to slither over the monkey's back, but the monkey jerked away, and she missed it. Vasanti growled in annoyance.

Sorry, Tana said. She found the tools and set to work. Unlike Kanvar's armor, which was made of individual blue scales affixed to leather, the king's armor was made whole from lesser green dragon hides. The green dragon scales were smaller and would be no good for sewing individually. But the lesser dragon hides had been expertly cured, scales and all, to be light and flexible, and a lot more practical for blending in than bright blue.

Tana finished the alterations before Vasanti returned with the meal for the wyrmlings. The armor, Amar's belt pouches, crossbow, and other gear felt strange on Tana, but she figured she'd need it. She tucked the singing stone in its iron box into one of the pouches. There was a loop on the belt for the jungle knife, but she kept it in hand for the time being.

Vasanti returned carrying three black monkeys. Tana was as hungry as the wyrmlings, but she stepped outside while Vasanti, her children, and Frost devoured the monkeys. Tana was glad Parmver had taught her good shielding techniques, since she had no desire to experience green dragon dining as if she were eating raw black monkey herself. Instead she gathered her own meal of mushrooms and fruit. She had just started to eat when Mani stepped out of the lair.

Mani shook her arms and wiggled her fingers as if trying to get blood to flow back through them. "I never want to be paralyzed like that again."

"I'm sorry, Your Majesty," Tana said. She held out some fruit to Mani who took it and sighed.

"I'll never see him again, Tana. You know that?"

"Probably not alive, no." Tana finished her fruit before speaking again. "Kanvar is sending Devaj to get you and Aadi and take you to be with my people. Eska and Denali are there. You won't be lonely."

"Oh, I'll be lonely."

Vasanti rumbled from inside the lair.

"Vasanti knows how you feel. She has been lonely, too, since she lost her mate." Tana took an idle swipe at a fern frond with the jungle knife.

Mani looked like she might start crying again, but somehow kept the tears back. "I'm sorry I fought with you, Tana. This isn't your fault. I hope I didn't hurt you."

Tana rubbed the scratch on her face from Mani's nails. She'd had more important things to worry about than a little scratch. "It's nothing. I . . . am going back to the palace tonight to try and free him again. Vasanti can climb the cliff."

"Tana, no." Mani grabbed her arm. "You were right. He gave himself up to keep the rest of us safe. Don't ruin that. Promise me you won't go."

Tana pulled away. "I have to."

"You'll have no chance against Rajahansa, Haidar, and Liander."

"I'm a Naga now. They can't control me."

"They are older than you and stronger, both physically and mentally."

"I'll sneak in at night. They won't see me."

"They'll feel you, and even if they are asleep and don't, you can be sure they'll have gold dragons awake and guarding him. You cannot do this. Come with Aadi and me to be with your people."

"I won't leave my dragon. She needs me. Even if I don't go to the palace, I must stay here and help her with the children. She doesn't have a mate, you know, and it's easier to hunt without them on her back. I'm happy in the deep jungle. I like it here. You go. Take care of Aadi. Amar said to tell you to care for him as if he were your own son."

"Sounds like a good idea." Devaj jumped down the last bit of hill to where the women were standing in front of the lair. "Is Aadi inside? Is he still paralyzed?"

"I'm right here." Aadi stumbled from the lair. "Stinking green dragon. Tana, I can't believe you bonded with her. You'll spend your whole life paralyzed."

"I don't think so." Tana rubbed the glistening green armor. "Vasanti and I will get along just fine." She grinned, but inside she wasn't smiling. Mani's warnings about Tana's plan to sneak into the palace made sense. The odds of her getting in, killing Amar, and getting back out without being discovered were slim. She could be killed, and that would kill Vasanti, and Vasanti's children would die of starvation or be eaten by some predator. Tana shook her head. There had to be a better way. With the gold dragons on guard, it would take a whole troop of dragon hunters to get into the palace and finish Rajahansa.

Tana bit her lip. She'd seen the dragon hunters coming in Kanvar's mind. Dragon hunters and soldiers. All they needed was to find the palace, and they'd have the strength to finish Rajahansa and Parmver's sons along with him. They didn't know the way to the palace . . . but Tana did.

"You think you can climb this hill now?" Devaj was asking Aadi.

Aadi rubbed his legs. "I'm sure going to try. I never want to meet a Great Green dragon again." He started up the hill, using tree branches and saplings to steady his ascent.

Mani started up after him. Frost darted out of the cave and flapped up the hill as well.

Devaj took Tana's hand. "Are you all right? You've been through too much. I hate to leave you here."

"I prefer to stay with my dragon. But, Devaj, will you do something for me?"

"Anything. What?"

"Could you fly me to the village? All my things are there, and I have certain comforts of home I'd like to bring back here with me. You don't have to stay. Vasanti will follow on the ground, and the two of us will come back to the lair together." Tana smiled pleadingly up at Devaj and squeezed his hand.

"Of course." Devaj kissed her hand. "But Elkatran will have all he can carry, plus one, in taking Mani and Aadi with me to the new village. Mani can ride behind me on his back. Elkatran will have to carry Aadi in his talons. Not too comfortable. Bensharie is with me, however. He's small and fast. He could take you there, but you'll have to get in and out quickly. The human armies have already reached the coast."

"I'll hurry, and Bensharie doesn't need to stay. Vasanti and I will be able to get out safer on the ground. Haidar's dragon armies will not attack a Great Green dragon."

"You hope."

"I know, or we'd already be dead." Tana gave Devaj another coaxing smile.

"All right. Come on then. Let's climb back up this dreadful hill. I can't wait to get back to the new village."

Devaj headed up the slope.

Vasanti crawled out of her lair and brushed up against Tana. *This is dangerous, what you're planning.*

Tana gave her a hug. I know. *But I have to try.*

Then I will meet you at the palace. Vasanti licked her face and crawled back into her lair.

Tana swiped at a couple of vines with her jungle knife just to loosen her muscles and fight back the fear that threatened to overwhelm her. Then she climbed up to find Bensharie.

Chapter Thirteen

Tana climbed up the slope to the rocks. The rockslide was difficult enough to climb that she didn't envy Kanvar trying to scale it to the gray cliffs above. Halfway up, the rain clouds that so often overshadowed the jungle rolled up to meet the cliffs, and a soft drizzle fell on her face and arms. She felt strange moving in the armor that clung to her skin as if she too were a dragon. But the armor didn't hamper her movement. The rain droplets glinted off the green scales. As she climbed, her body regained more strength than she had felt in days. The dragon sickness was behind her now, and she thrived on not just her own strength and vitality but Vasanti's as well.

When the rockslide came above the treetops, she found Bensharie waiting for her on his haunches against the cliff face, wings folded. She'd seen many gold dragons in the palace, but had not been introduced to any but the young females Rajahansa had chosen for her to bond with. The dragons seemed much the same to her, and she'd only been able to tell them apart by her sense of their being. As she looked up at Bensharie, she realized she recognized his sense of self. He was the poet, the romanticist that lived in a hall not far from the chambers where the women liked to meet and talk. He was also the dragon who had braved the lesser volcanic dragon to save Tana and Kanvar.

Tana waved a greeting to him, but kept her mind shielded from his. She could not have Bensharie sensing her fear and resolve to do what she must. If she wanted a quick ride to the village, she had to play that her motives were other than her true plan.

Greetings, Bensharie said, bowing to her. *Are you sure whatever is at the village is very important? It's rather dangerous going back there. Rajahansa believes the humans know the way to the village, and he has planned a surprise attack on their forces when they reach it.*

"He's setting a trap for the human armies?" Tana reached Bensharie's side and stood there uncomfortably wondering how she was supposed to mount him, and what was the polite way to ask him to let her.

A large bulk of Haidar's army is hidden around the village. The dragons are hungry. He hasn't let them feed. Bensharie shook himself as if revolted by Haidar's actions. *As soon as the dragon hunters pull out their singing stones, the dragons will go into a wild frenzy. And this is where you want to go? Right into the jaws of the trap to pick up a few trinkets? I don't know how you convinced Devaj this was a good idea.*

"Bensharie." Tana reached out a tentative hand and touched his leg. The golden plates were smooth and slicked with rain. "I don't want to put you in any danger. Never mind. I'll have Vasanti go with me."

Along the jungle floor? That's crazy. You'll be killed.

"It's very important to me that I reach the village, and Vasanti is a force to be reckoned with."

Even if the lesser dragons are afraid of her, the humans won't be. I've seen the army. There are thousands of soldiers. She'll be killed.

"You worry too much, Bensharie. Devaj thought it was all right for me to go, especially if you fly me there before the humans arrive." Tana rubbed his leg and looked pleadingly into his face.

Bensharie ruffled his wings. *I'll take you, but I won't leave you there alone. You get your things quickly, and I'll fly you back out.*

"I won't be alone." She didn't want to tell Bensharie anything of her plans, but she could tell she had to give him something to think about. "I'll be with Karishi. He's inside the mountain by the village, isn't he? Once he's sealed the passages, the human armies won't be able to get to him. They won't even know he's there."

He's already sealed himself in.

"But he will open the passages for me. Bensharie, I'm sure you're too young to understand this, but sometimes there is great affection between a man and a woman. He left the palace so suddenly I didn't even get a chance to say goodbye. I need to see him. I want to be with him now."

Bensharie turned his head away from Tana and let out an agitated puff of gold sparkles. *I thought you and Kanvar were considering mating?*

"Mating?" Tana's face burned. "Kanvar and I are friends, and I'm not mating with anyone just yet. Humans aren't like that. We . . . take time to get to know each other, fall in love, get married. And right now, I need some time with Karishi."

I think Kanvar would be jealous.

"Bensharie, are you going to fly me to the village or not? Because if you're not, I have a long way to cover on foot." Tana stalked away from him and headed back down the rocks.

No wait, I'll take you. I've faced human soldiers before. I just don't want anything bad to happen to you. Bensharie hunched down so Tana could climb onto his back. He was small compared to many of the other dragons, but much the same size as the dragons Rajahansa would have had Tana bond with.

She slid onto his back. As he raised his head, the gold plate in front of her locked into place over her lap, keeping her secure. Bensharie launched into the air, and she was flying. She could not deny the smooth beauty of gold dragon flight. Indeed, she'd given that up by bonding with Vasanti, but did not regret her choice.

You and Karishi, Bensharie muttered. *I never saw that coming.*

Tana forced a laugh through her teeth and answered with her mind since the wind of their flight would have covered the sound of her voice. *You have to admit he's handsome.*

Kanvar's handsome.

Tana's heart twisted. Yes, Kanvar was handsome, and brave and passionate and busy trying to keep Rajahansa from taking his father to Stonefountain—a task he needed her help for. In fact, Tana had no attraction to Karishi. He'd seemed more like a father figure to her in her brief interactions with him at the palace.

You and Kanvar are good friends, it seems? she said to Bensharie.

Yes. We've been through a lot together.

Bensharie's flight took them around the mountains and back toward the coast. Soon, Tana could see the Black River snaking below her from the peaks that shrouded the palace, across the jungle floor, to the village, and from there out to the walls of the Maran colony and the ocean. The bay next to the colony was alive with ships. Long boats carried soldiers to shore where they were marshaling into ranks. The Maran soldiers in one group and the Varnan soldiers in another. The dragon hunters from both countries clumped in knots here and there on the beach.

Can they see us? Tana asked.

Bensharie grimaced inwardly. *It's cloudy. They can see us, if they're looking. But we're too far away for their weapons to do anything.* Bensharie turned away from the coast, flew around the arm of the mountain out of view of the ocean, and landed on the ledge in the cliffs above the village.

The round copper plate for calling the Nagas from the palace that had always graced the landing was gone without a trace.

Bensharie bent down so Tana could slide off his back. Her green dragonscale boots crunched against the stone. "Fly now, Bensharie. I'll see you later."

Bensharie shook his head. *Not until I see you safely with Karishi.*

"Fine." Tana walked over to the cliffs and pressed her hands against the pocked black rock that had spurted from a volcano long ago. If Karishi had already sealed himself in, there was only one way she could join him. She sent her mind out looking for Karishi's. She didn't know it as well as Kanvar's, and felt uncomfortable probing a mountain of stone for thoughts of life.

Tana? Karishi's surprised thought came into her mind. *What are you doing here? Everyone is supposed to be gone away safe.*

I need to talk to you. Let me in.

Karishi's mind brushed through hers until he could look through her eyes to be sure she was not surrounded by soldiers and dragon hunters.

Seeing her alone with Bensharie, he withdrew the penetrating thoughts back to the level of simple communication. *Stay there, I'll be up in a minute.*

"He's coming." Tana told Bensharie.

Bensharie snorted.

Tana paced back and forth across the ledge, trying to reduce her anxiety while she waited. Her plan was desperate, crazy. She couldn't be sure Karishi would even help her. But she had to try. When she thought of the evil Rajahansa had already perpetrated under Khalid's influence she could hardly imagine what horrors the world would see if Khalid returned to it fully.

Though there was no sign of an entrance, the rock face split with a grind and tap of stone on stone until a vertical crack opened just large enough that Tana could squeeze through it if she turned sideways.

Karishi slipped out of the crack, carrying a torch and greeted Tana and Bensharie. Water condensed on the copper scale armor that clung to his muscled form. Blond streaks highlighted his brown hair. His face, neither young nor old, looked haunted. His eyes troubled. She sensed he had left his home in Darvat in hopes of a better place, but now with the human armies bearing down on him, he wished he'd never come here. She felt sorry for him. He'd been so lonely all his life, and found only solitude again.

"Karishi." Tana reached out and laid a trembling hand against his chest.

Surprised, Karishi pressed his own hand on top of hers. She had never reached out to him before.

Well, I'll leave you to your romance then, Bensharie said. *Don't stay out on the cliff long. The humans are coming.* He launched into the air and sped away.

"Romance?" Karishi said, a touch of scarlet creeping into his face.

Tana frowned and pulled her hand away. She didn't want Karishi to get the wrong idea. "I just told him what I had to in order to get him to bring me here." She edged past Karishi and slid through the crack in the cliff to a narrow passageway beyond. The ceiling of the tunnel was low, almost brushing the top of her head. The walls were only inches away from her shoulders. The floor was rough rock. It was a primitive tunnel, cluttered with debris as if Karishi had just created it.

Letting out a disappointed *tsk*, Karishi followed her inside. "Too bad. I wouldn't mind a bit of romance just now." He held his hand, palm out, toward the crack in the rock leading back outside.

Tana held her breath as she waited for Karishi to manipulate the stone back in place. She opened her mind and tried to see into his to learn how to use her powers to move the rock. Though her intent was to learn to open not close, she hoped witnessing how Karishi did it would help her.

Karishi repulsed her from his mind and snapped his shields up. "What are you doing?"

"I have to learn how to manipulate the rock. I need to be able to get back into the palace." Tana ran her fingers along the stone.

"Why?"

Tana hesitated while she rebuilt her own shields. She didn't know if she could trust Karishi with the true nature of her cause. It would sound wrong no matter how she said it aloud. Better to be careful. "His Majesty asked me to do something for him."

Karishi moved up close enough to her that she could feel the heat of his chest. He placed his hand down on the rock next to hers so their fingers overlapped.

Tana flushed, uncomfortable being so close to a man after her encounters with Haidar and Liander.

"I meant, why do you need to manipulate rock to get back into the palace? It is your home." The torch in his other hand guttered in a breeze that wafted in through the crack.

"I-I . . . ran away."

"That doesn't seem wise."

"No, you don't understand. Haidar planned to force me to marry him against my will. He would have. He got into my head and twisted my thoughts all around, trying to make me willing to accept his advances." Tana shuddered and pulled away, freeing her hand from Karishi's once again.

Karishi shook his head. "I can't believe he would do such a thing."

Tana balled her hands into fists. "Belive it. He messed with my mind and struck me with his fist. And Liander held me bound and kissed me against my will. You can ask His Majesty. He witnessed Liander's assault, but he could not do anything to stop it." Tana told herself to stop talking. She didn't need to spill everything out, but her anger welled up inside her.

"He's the king. Of course, he could stop it."

"No. Didn't Devaj tell you? Rajahansa bound his mind and chained him to the wall. Liander threatened to kill Mani, if His Majesty tried to escape or help me." Pulling up all her courage, Tana pressed a shaking hand against Karishi's chest. "Karishi, when I tried to free the king, Parmver claimed responsibility for my actions and Rajahansa stabbed his claw through Parmver's chest."

"No." Karishi's sharp voice cut through the dimness in the cave. His face twisted into a frown. "You must be wrong."

"I'm not wrong. Rajahansa killed Parmver, and I ran away and bonded with a Great Green dragon. But King Amar made me promise him I'd come back to free him. I need to be able to open the rock face to get into Parmver's lab below the palace. It's the only way. Please teach me how to do it."

"Manipulating rock is not something you can learn in a moment or even a day. It took me decades."

"Did you have someone to teach you?"

"No. I had to learn it myself, slowly and carefully. And I got my hands stuck in the rock for several days once, scraped all the skin off the tips of my fingers another time, and crushed one of my hands so bad I couldn't use it for a long time. Air is forgiving. Water is forgiving. Stone is not."

"Please, just let me watch you do it. I'm sure I can figure it out."

"No. You can't."

"Let me try."

"All right." Karishi touched the rock and it ground back together, sealing the crack and blocking her from the outside world. Tana had meant to try to follow his thoughts as he worked, but he did it so fast, she didn't catch more than a passing wisp of something she didn't understand.

"Go ahead and try," Karishi said.

Tana took a deep breath. "Is there air in here? It's like the whole mountain has closed in around us. I can't breathe."

"Of course there is air. The torch would go out if there wasn't." Karishi waved the torch, which still burned with a merry yellow flame. "You needn't worry. I've put in air vents."

"All right." Trying to fight back the panic of being sealed underground, Tana put her hand on the rock and pictured in her mind how it had looked when Karishi had opened it.

Nothing happened.

"Thinking isn't enough," Karishi said. "Imagining isn't enough, though it's a start. You have to be able to sense the rock, connect with it, and then force it to obey your commands."

"How can that be? A rock is not living like a human or an animal. I can't *sense* it."

"And that is why you will never be able to make it obey you." Karishi reopened the crack. "Call Bensharie back and have him fly you to the palace."

"We'll be seen."

"Oh, and you think you won't be seen if you tear open the rock below the palace? You probably noticed, the process isn't quiet. Besides, once you do get inside, how do you intend to free the king? Rajahansa, Haidar and Liander are all more powerful than you, and they have all the gold dragons on their side. You have no hope of accomplishing anything but getting caught."

"You could help me."

"Oh, no. I'm staying out of this mess. If I could, I'd go back to Darvat right now. This place is nothing like Devaj led me to believe." Karishi pointed to the crack. "Go out and do whatever you want, or stay here with me if you want. Either way, I won't be opening this tunnel again for a very long time. I've stored enough food and water to last a very long time."

"Karishi, you can't just hide and do nothing."

"Oh yes I can. The question is, do you want to stay safe here with me, or do you want to go back out there and get yourself killed?"

Gritting her teeth, Tana slipped through the crack to the outside. Coming out of the darkness felt like a heavy weight lifting off her. She knew she could never stand to live underground the way Karishi did. She rested her fingers against the rough stone. "I have to *sense* the rock?"

"Everything in the world has a presence. People and animals are always moving, doing, and thinking so it's easier to feel them. Plants move a little slower, and they don't think, but you can feel them seeking for rain and sunlight. Rocks are . . . different. They do not grow; they exist. They do not *want* anything; they just are. If you would learn to sense the rocks, you must learn patience. You must learn to sit beside them for hours, days, weeks. You must learn to stop moving and silence your own thoughts."

"I don't have time for that. I ask you again to come help me."

Karishi shook his head. "I am a rock. I have the patience of this mountain. The rocks know if they wait, all that moves about them will change. This is not my fight. Goodbye, Tana. Try not to get yourself killed." Karishi waved his hand, and with a scrape and grind the rocks closed up between them.

Chapter Fourteen

Tana stared for a long moment at the blank cliff face where the crack had been. She put her hand against the rock and tried to sense it like she would Kanvar's presence. She sensed nothing. Dropping her hand, she turned away and cast her senses down into the jungle.

Bensharie had not exaggerated. Among the trees and along the jungle floor thousands of hungry lesser dragons, snakes, black monkeys, even birds waited for the human invasion. Far more than Haidar had sent against her and Amar that morning. It was as if the whole jungle waited in frozen silence like a Great Green dragon, motionless above its prey.

There were so many humans and so many dragons, she couldn't guess who would win the battle. One thing was for sure, a lot of people and dragons would die. It's a trap, Tana thought. The humans will come here and never get past this place. Even if they subdue the dragon army, they won't know how to get to the palace. I'm the only one who knows the way. The humans don't know it, but they need me. I have to warn them about this trap, and I need them to help me stop Rajahansa.

Behind the rain clouds, the sun dipped toward the horizon. She felt exposed on the cliff ledge and hurried down the stone steps to the village. It lay silent in the falling darkness, like a dead thing, the spirit of life gone from it, her people vanished. Her skin prickled beneath her armor. The day Kanvar had killed Mahanth, she'd forbidden Kanvar from taking the Great Green dragon's stone, warning him that the village would be cursed if he took it. He'd left it alone then, but villagers who went to bury the body later said that Mahanth's dragonstone had been removed. Had Kanvar done it, or some other unscrupulous person? Either way, the curse had fallen, dooming the village.

Staying away from the hut that used to be her home, she crossed the high walkways to the platform overlooking the Black River. Upstream from the village there were waterfalls and rapids that made boating on it dangerous, but downstream the water flowed smoothly. Long ago, before the Maranies came, the villagers used to travel often to the ocean to gather sea shells and hunt salt water fish. Though the villagers no longer went as far as the Maran colony, they still used the river for fishing and traveling. Several long boats made from hollowed out trees lay waiting on the platform overlooking the river.

Tana lowered the smallest boat down to the jungle floor then descended and put it onto the water. She climbed in then pushed off from the bank.

The still water lapped against the side of the boat as she drifted downstream along the turns through the emerald blackness of the jungle. The sun set. She could feel the dragons in the trees on either side and serpents swimming in the water. Hungry. Held in check by Haidar's mind. The ones that smelled her or saw her did not attack. They'd been commanded to watch for human armies not jungle villagers. But she was dressed in armor like a dragon hunter and didn't look like a villager. The dragons stirred and considered attacking her, but she nudged their minds back away. She was a villager. She impressed the images of a simple villager on their minds and they let her float down toward the shore. Her real danger lay with the humans. They would have singing stones.

She pressed her hand against the pouch on the supply belt. Parmver's singing stone waited there. She needed the soldiers to let her live long enough to talk to their leaders. She had to steel herself against the song of the stones so she could pretend they didn't affect her until she had a chance to share her plan, though that plan was severely curtailed by the fact that she couldn't offer them a way into the palace. She could get them there, but they'd have to scale a cliff face guarded by gold dragons to reach the palace itself.

Could they do it? She didn't know. But she had to try to ask them. She had to warn them about the trap. Would they not suspect a fight? Did they know how many Nagas there were? Surely they expected a fight or they wouldn't have sailed with such a mighty force, but the fight would be all for naught if they didn't have anyone to tell them where the palace was. They could wander Kundiland jungles for a long time before ever finding it.

If not for the threat of Khalid, she would let them do it. If she had not witnessed first hand Khalid's evil, she would not be sure his return to the world was such a bad thing. If she had not promised the king to stop him from being taken over by Khalid's spirit, she could just go back to Vasanti's lair and live in peace. Let the human armies languish in the jungle. But no. The duty rested on her shoulders to stop Khalid.

None of the other Nagas would be willing to sacrifice Naga lives to keep the world free. Well, Kanvar would surely sacrifice his own, but not his father's.

An hour on the water, followed by another, brought her round and in view of the Maran colony. The black stone walls were lit with torches. Solders stood guard there. In the fields around the colony, the armies had set camp for the night. The cry of singing stones filled the air and grew sharper as her boat drew closer. Watch fires flickered along the shoreline. Armed sentries stood out as sharp silhouettes against the flames. She doubted she could sneak past them, and she didn't dare try.

Her hands tingled with fear. Her senses sharpened so she could hear the sound of the men's voices above the croak and hum of the night jungle. The smell of camdors and men and armor and bovinder roasting on the fires sent alarms through her. Here were enemies. Humans come to kill the Nagas, and she was a Naga. They would kill her. For a moment she sat paralyzed with fear that they would shoot her in the dark without ever giving her a chance to explain.

"Halt. Who's there?"

The sharp cry from shore jerked her hand in motion. She pulled the iron box from her belt pouch and opened it. The blue glow of the stone lit her face as she lifted it out so the sentries on shore could see it. Its song joined with so many others already screaming on the beach. She would have no power here. But having just bonded, the lack of power did not bother her so much. She didn't know how to use it anyway for more than to sense the presence of jungle animals and stay in contact with Vasanti's mind. Her link to Vasanti was severed by the wail of the stone. She shivered and then pushed the pain and fear away to speak.

"My name is Tana," She called out. "I'm a dragon hunter. I need to speak with your leader. I'm on your side."

Rushed whispers sounded among the sentries then a call sounded for her to come to shore.

She set to work with the paddle and brought the boat up to the bank close to the watch fire. A couple of men grabbed the front of the boat and dragged it up onto the bank. Tana stepped out, aware of how she must look dressed in green dragon hunter armor, with the crossbow harness and belt pouches and jungle knife. Surely she looked like a dragon hunter, with singing stone and all. She slid the stone back into the box in her pouch and greeted the soldiers.

"Sorry to come in so late. I've scouted up the river and come back with important news."

"You don't look like them that went up the river this afternoon."

"No, of course not. I've been hunting this vicinity for a couple of years now and have a camp upriver where I live. If your men have not come back when you expected them to, they may be dead. There is great danger up this river. I need to speak to your leader." Tana glanced from the walls of the colony to the two camps of soldiers to the smaller camps of various groups of dragon hunters. "Who is in charge? Never in my life did I think to see Maran and Varnan hunters and soldiers in such close vicinity to each other without being in battle against each other."

The soldiers grimaced. One spat on the ground. "We have a common foe. Do you realize there are Nagas here?"

Tana snorted and patted her pouch with the singing stone. "I know of the Nagas. They've stayed hidden for a long time. I haven't needed this stone until recently. The past few weeks the Nagas have been more active. Something has stirred them out of hiding. I wasn't sure what until I noticed your arrival."

"You've lived here for so long, and they haven't bothered you?"

"The Nagas have been here since the fall of Stonefountain and haven't bothered anyone. Ask the Maran soldiers that settled this colony. The Nagas have been quiescent until now."

"And now?"

"I suppose they feel threatened by your invasion." Tana smiled at the irony of that and fingered her jungle knife. If the humans had not feared the Nagas and come to destroy them, then Rajahansa, Haidar, and Liander would have likely been content to stay hidden in their palace for another thousand years instead of calling on Khalid to help them. "But we're wasting time. I have urgent news for your leader. I know where the Nagas are, and I can lead you to them. I also know where they have laid their trap to destroy you."

"Very well, come with me." One of the soldiers motioned for Tana to follow him and strode away from the river, across the army encampments in the fields to the Maran Colony proper.

Tana's heart beat in fear and her head spun from the sound of so many singing stones wailing their torment to the night. But she kept her stride steady and confident. I am a dragon hunter, she told herself. A dragon hunter not a Naga.

They entered the main gate and went into a building just beyond. The room inside was lit with oil lamps along the walls, and four men sat at a table that was spread with maps and uncleared dishes from a late meal. There was a gray-haired Maran soldier in blue dragonhide armor and a gold general's braid on his shoulder. A younger man, more the age of Tana's father, wore tan leather armor emblazoned with the Varnan crest, that of a shattered fountain. These men wore swords at their sides and carried themselves like solders.

The other two men were dragon hunters, one with the dark hair and pale skin of the Maranies, and the other with the sun-bronzed Varnan complexion. The Varnan was old, wrinkled, with gray hair braided down his back. His dragonhide armor was worn but well cared for. This was a man of action, who even in his senior years did not wear armor just to look impressive. The armor, though in perfect repair, showed signs of recent and continual use. He was a dragon hunter who had never stopped hunting. And this man stiffened the moment Tana stepped into the room. The next moment he was up from his chair and had his crossbow free from its harness, loaded, and pointing at Tana.

Tana pulled her fingers away from her jungle knife and spread her hands.

"Is there a problem, Qadim?" The Maran general asked.

"She's a Naga," Qadim said, then turned his anger on the soldier that had accompanied her. "You brought a Naga into our headquarters. I ordered you to keep the singing stones free."

"No, sir." The soldier said, taking a step back from the angry dragon hunter. "This is Tana. She can't be a Naga. She has a singing stone of her own and had it unboxed as she approached. She said she's a dragon hunter who has been hunting this area for some time. She claims to know where the Nagas are and of an ambush they have set for us."

Qadim snorted. "Chandran, your men are idiots." He came around the table and pressed the tip of the crossbow against Tanas chest over her heart. "Give me one good reason I shouldn't shoot you this instant, Naga." He had his own singing stone hanging loose around his neck. Its voice was a guttural male shout of agony.

"I know everything about every single Naga in Kundiland. I know where they live. I know what each of them is doing right now. And I want to help you." Tana's voice shook, though she tried to stay steady and calm.

"Why would you betray your own kind?" Qadim's eyes flashed and his finger inched closer to the trigger.

General Chandran rose, came to Qadim's side, and put a restraining hand on the crossbow. "Qadim, before you kill her, why don't you tell me what makes you so sure she's a Naga. She doesn't look like one. She doesn't act like one. She carries a singing stone, for goodness sake."

Qadim let out a dark laugh. "I *know* she's a Naga because I *know* the armor and weapons she wears. They belong to Amar, the Naga who married Kumar Raza's daughter. The Naga who fooled the most elite men in this world into thinking he was a dragon hunter. I will not be tricked again, and certainly not by someone wearing Amar's armor."

General Chandran stared at Tana with penetrating eyes. "Is this true?" he asked her.

Tana steeled herself. She knew that coming here could end her life, but the chance of success had been worth the risk. "Yes. I am a Naga, and this is the king's armor."

"King?" Qadim said. His gnarled hand trembled on the crossbow. The two men that had remained seated until now jumped to their feet.

Tana nodded. "You see, there are things I know that you don't. Important information that is vital to your survival."

"Why have you come here?" Chandran asked. "You should know that any lies you tell us will not save your friends."

"I came because His Majesty, Amar, Grandson of Khalid, wants you to know that the world is in jeopardy. The danger is far greater than you have yet imagined." Tana's eyes burned and she fought to hold back unwanted tears. She had to be strong, now, at this decisive moment.

"You're crying?" General Chandran said incredulously.

Tana tried to say more. To tell what had to be said, but a lump rose in her throat, choking back the words for a second.

Chandran frowned. "Ease off, Qadim. She's only a child, can't you see that? And a girl."

"She's a Naga," Qadim said, loathing in his voice, but he stepped back a few feet.

The Varnan general cleared his throat. "Are you saying that the royal line survived the fall of Stonefountain? It's not possible."

"It is. Let me show you how." Tana eased her hand down toward the pouch that held Parmver's singing stone.

Qadim tensed, and the Maran dragon hunter drew out his own crossbow.

"It's only a pouch, not a weapon, at least not one that can hurt *you*." Tana eased open the pouch and pulled out the little iron box that housed Parmver's singing stone.

"How could a singing stone have saved the royal line?" Chandran said. "It was the stones that facilitated the overthrow of Stonefountain."

"If you let me live long enough, I'll explain." Tana tipped the box so the stone rolled out on the table. "Such a small stone. So small compared to Akshara's. The smallest stone for the poorest of human slaves in that dreadful city. There was a Naga whose name was Parmver. Once a friend and advisor to the king, he was an alchemist specializing in medicines, which he harvested from plants in the Kundiland jungle. As the king spiraled into evil, rejecting Parmver's counsel to free the slaves and treat the humans with respect, Parmver spent more and more of his time in his lab here in Kundiland. When a terrible plague swept through the city, Parmver found a cure and brought it back to Stonefountain. He meant it for all the city's residents, but King Khalid took the whole supply for the Nagas.

"Pamver argued with him, but the king refused to see reason. Cast out of the king's presence and left with only one drought of the medicine for his own use, Parmver went down into the city, intending to find and save the life of at least one person. A desperate slave came to him, begging the medicine to save the life of his daughter. The slave offered the box with the singing stone in exchange. Parmver needed no payment for giving the medicine as he had intended to do, but the man ran away, leaving the box in Parmver's hands. Parmver opened it and realized in shock what the stone could do and what that meant for the Nagas. But by then the city was already moving, gathering for the uprising. Parmver had been banished from the king's presence. He had no time to warn anyone. Yet he acted swiftly, abducting the king's young son from the nursery and flying him here to Kundiland."

Tana swallowed.

The men stared at her as if her story were something so horrible that they never could have imagined it on their own. Since they said nothing, Tana continued.

"Parmver raised the child as his own, and taught him to be everything that Khalid had not been: kind, patient, concerned with serving others instead of being served. Eventually Parmver had three Naga sons and a daughter. He taught them the same code of honor. The oldest of his sons was killed by a human he thought was a friend. The other two boys built a golden palace, a smaller replica of the palace at Stonefountain, and the family lived there in peace for hundreds of years. Parmver's daughter married the king's son, and the two had a son. Amar, who it seems you have met." Tana nodded to Qadim then continued.

"Amar's parents were killed by dragon hunters, but he did not retaliate against those who had killed them. Having been trained by Parmver, he wished only to live in peace with the world. I have met him. He is selfless. And this key point is the most important for you to understand. He would willingly lay down his life for the lives and safety of every man present here, dragon hunters and soldiers alike. And that is why I have come to you. He has asked me to kill him, and I can't do it on my own."

"Hold on," Chandran said. "Your story made sense until that last bit. By the fountain, why would the king want us to kill him?"

"You say 'by the fountain' and on that account you are correct. It is Stonefountain that is your greatest threat now." Tana shuddered. The constant wail of the singing stones made her dizzy.

"Why?" the Varnan general demanded.

Tana stumbled over to the table and sat down un-invited. Better that than fall down. "Do you know why the stones sing? Do you understand what they are?"

"They are stones filled with the magic of Stonefountain," Qadim said.

"They are more than that. They are the spirits of the dead that once resided at Stonefountain. They scream because when their souls were torn from the fountain, they were consigned to agony."

"Ridiculous," the Varnan general said.

Scowling, General Chandran raised a hand to silence his Varnan counterpart. "No, General Zetan. It's true. I have personal witness of it. The fountain hosts the spirits of the dead. But what does this have to do with Amar?"

Tana shivered again. Though the night was hot, cold chills prickled her arms. "King Khalid is dead. His spirit is in the fountain. And not long ago, Amar's oldest son—you know Amar had two Naga sons, Devaj and Kanvar? Yes? Good—Devaj took a singing stone to the fountain intent on freeing the spirit trapped in the stone from its torment. As Devaj put his hand into the water, Khalid's spirit grabbed him and held him. He raked across Devaj's mind, stealing all knowledge of our world now. Worse, he formed a link with Devaj's thoughts, a link which he used to communicate with Amar's dragon, Rajahansa."

General Zetan swore. The other men shifted uncomfortably, their faces clouding with anger and concern.

Tana forced herself to continue speaking. It all came down to this. "When Rajahansa and Parmver's two sons learned of your imminent attack, they turned to the one person they thought might know how to save them."

"Khalid," Chandran said. His fists clenched and red flooded his face.

"Yes, Khalid. And Khalid has promised them sure victory against you for a price."

"What price?" Qadim asked, venom in his voice.

"Khalid wants a body so he can return to the living world. Rajahansa agreed to give him Amar's. Amar fought him, fought his own dragon, mind, body, and soul. With Parmver's and my help, Amar escaped from the palace where his own dragon had him chained. Rajahansa killed Parmver in retaliation. Parmver's sons made no move to stop their father's murder. Their fear of your invasion has turned them to more evil than I would have dared imagine. That poor, dear, old man, his life snuffed out in front of me. And I and Aadi, another young man from my village, left at the mercy of those three turned to evil: Rajahansa, Haidar, and Liander. I will not tell you what they did to me, but I escaped them. Aadi was not so lucky, and he became the object of their . . . I cannot hardly explain to you what they planned for Aadi. It was a perversion above all perverseness. Rajahansa tried to force a bond with Aadi against his will and use him to sacrifice to Khalid instead of Amar. When Amar learned of this treachery, he agreed to give himself up to Rajahansa in exchange for Aadi's freedom."

"Amar or this other boy, either way Khalid returns," Qadim said. His crossbow was no longer pointed at Tana, but his hands shook on the weapon.

Tana's hands shook as well, and she clasped them together to try to still them. "Before Amar gave himself up, he left me his armor and a charge. I must make sure that Rajahansa does not bring him to Stonefountain, whatever it takes. He has ordered me to kill him. That is the only way to free him from slavery to his own dragon and insure that Khalid does not walk this world once more."

Chapter Fifteen

Tana finished speaking. She still felt chilled, though the room was stuffy, hot, and smelled of lamp oil and human sweat. Had she said too much, she wondered, or not enough?

Frowning, General Chandran ran his fingers through his gray hair.

After a moment General Zetan slammed his fist on the table. "It's a lie meant to draw us away to Stonefountain right when we have our prey trapped here."

Tana shook her head. "My intent is not to send you running to Stonefountain. My wish is to show you where the palace is and have you help me kill the king. I love him, he's like a father to me, but I know that the only freedom he has left is in death."

"It'll be a trap then," the Varnan dragon hunter said.

"Haidar and Rajahansa *have* laid a trap for you," Tana said. "They think you are coming to the jungle village where I was born. The ambush lies there, or it was a few hours ago when I left the place." Tana explained about the starving dragons that waited for the human armies upriver.

General Chandran put a hand on Tana's shoulder, squeezing it like a raptor's talon. "Let's pretend just for a moment that we believe you. What is your plan?"

Tana shuddered. "That's the problem. I know where the palace is, but I don't know how to get you there safely, or even how to get you inside. There's an army of dragons in the jungle. There's an entire Great Gold dragon pride guarding the palace. But worse, the palace is built on a cliff, thousands of feet above the canopy. There used to be an entrance down lower with steps carved up to it, but that has been sealed."

"How did you escape?" Qadim asked.

"I jumped out the window. They have big windows for the dragons to fly in and out of. I fashioned myself a pair of wings, and I jumped."

"Your dragon couldn't just fly you?"

Tana thought of Vasanti and a smile crept onto her face. "My dragon does not fly. She is a Great Green dragon, a beautiful creature beyond measure. A matriarch of the jungle. Rajahansa is furious about that, of course. He doesn't think Nagas should bond to anyone but gold dragons. He's never forgiven Kanvar for bonding with his worst enemy, the leader of the Great Blue dragon pride. He blames all this mess on Kanvar and his dragon."

"Kanvar?" Qadim said. "Amar's crippled boy?"

"Yes. He considers Kanvar a traitor because Kanvar risked your discovering the Nagas here by going to stop the unknown Naga who had taken over the Maran government. You may think Kanvar is your enemy, but he's not. He risked his own life and the wellbeing of all the other Nagas to try to save your people."

"Kanvar's dead," Chandran snapped. "I personally put my sword through his gut and tossed his body into the ocean. I have many witnesses to that fact."

Tana sucked in a breath but couldn't do more than blink at Chandran in consternation. She'd just been with Kanvar that afternoon. Perhaps it would be best not to mention that. "I guess he did give his life then. For you, to help you, and you repaid him by killing him." Tana gripped the handle of her jungle knife. "I suppose you will kill me now as well."

"Not until you tell us where this palace is," General Zetan snapped.

"I think perhaps for the sake of my life I should lead you to it rather than just tell you," Tana said.

"You think that will save you in the end? If you're willing to betray your own people, what's to keep you from betraying us as well?" the Varnan general said.

"I serve my king. I follow his commands, and I will never betray that trust even if it means my own life is forfeit like Kanvar's was."

"Silence, both of you," General Chandran said. "I need to think for a moment." Chandran paced around the table in the ensuing silence. When he came back around to Tana, he stopped. "There are other Nagas. Tell me exactly who they are, where they are, and what they are doing."

"The Nagas are split. Rajahansa, Haidar, and Liander are at the palace, plotting to release Khalid. Amar's son Devaj has worked tirelessly to move the innocent jungle villagers to safety so they will not be killed in the coming fight. I spoke with him this afternoon, and he is far away helping the villagers resettle. He is a peaceable man and no threat to you. If he had any guts, he'd realize the predicament his father is in and help me."

"Help you kill his own father?" Chandran said, raising his eyebrows.

"Devaj didn't even stay at the palace to try to free his father. When things went bad, Devaj flew away. I believe Amar ordered him to save the villagers and stay with them to keep him out of the fighting."

"What about Karishi?" General Chandran asked.

"You know Karishi?" Tana said, surprised.

"We've met. His metallic serpent had the good grace not to eat me even though I invaded his lair. But I would have killed Karishi on the spot if his dragon had not protected him. Swords and crossbow bolts aren't much help against a metal dragon."

"No, I suppose not." Tana smiled at the thought of General Chandran face-to-face with Tazeran.

"Why are you smiling?" Qadim demanded.

Tana's smile widened. "Devaj brought Karishi to the palace, but his dragon made havoc with the gold. He licked it off of everything. If he'd been allowed to carry on, he would have been as gold as the Great Gold dragons and there wouldn't be a drop of gold leafing left on anything in the palace. He was such a naughty serpent, Karishi took him away to live hidden in some other mountain somewhere in Kundiland. Last I saw Karishi, I tried to get him to side with me, but he refused to take any side. He was headed deep underground with supplies to last forever. I think he doesn't mean to come back to the surface until several generations of humans have passed away."

"Who else?" Chandran asked.

"Well, me."

"And?"

"There aren't any others that I know of. I'm the youngest. I just bonded today."

"What about this Aadi you spoke of?" Qadim asked.

"He's not a Naga. Not yet. Parmver took him to the palace because he seemed to have some affinity with the dragons, but he hasn't come down with the dragon sickness. Rajahansa tried to force the fever on him, but it wouldn't come. Only time will tell if he is, in fact, a Naga or not. But he's with Devaj and the villagers. As far as I know, the only Nagas at the palace are Amar, Haidar, and Liander."

"What about the Naga we caught in Maran. Who was he?" Qadim asked.

"I have no idea. None of the Nagas at the palace knew anything about him. If you caught him, why didn't you just kill him?" Tana said.

"I told you, I personally hunted that Naga, Qadim," Chandran said. "But Kumar Raza beat me to him and finished him before I got there. At least, *that one* won't be a problem."

Tana pressed her lips together and wondered yet again what Chandran was playing at. Did he know Kumar Raza had Naga blood? Tana rose to her feet. "Well, I have told you all I know. Will you help me get into the palace and kill the king or not?"

"Oh, we're going to kill the king, all right," the Qadim said. "And you, and every other Naga in this cursed land."

"So be it," Tana said. "I only hope you succeed before Khalid returns. I do not think this world will be a very pleasant place to live in if he does. Oh, you may want to know, the Great Blue dragons have Akshara's singing stone and have been doing everything in their power to counter Rajahansa's actions. They know Rajahansa is bound for Stonefountain, and have made a vow to stop him. But their attacks on the palace have been, as of yet, unfruitful. The golds and the blues are too evenly matched."

"Nonsense," General Zetan said. "How could a gold dragon possibly stop a blue one?"

General Chandran laughed. "You've never witnessed the affect of gold dragon joy breath, have you? No, the golds are a force to be reckoned with. One we're going to have to figure out how to overcome." Chandran sat down across the table from Tana. "Can you contact the blue dragons? They could fly a small assault team up the cliffs to the palace while our main forces are engaged with the trap they expect us to fall into."

Tana rubbed her head. "I'd have to move away from the singing stones to try. I'm not sure if they'll listen. They hate Nagas more than you do."

"I think it's worth a try," Chandran said.

"You fought those dragons for a long time," Tana said. "They're not likely to forget that."

"Yes, but now we have a common foe, Khalid. I think you could make them see the necessity of our actions." Chandran rose and looked to the other three leaders in the room. "What say you? Do we trust the girl and ally ourselves with the blue dragons to mount a surprise attack on the palace, or do we push upriver as planned, conquering as we go, and hope we stumble upon the Nagas' lair?"

Tana held her breath. General Chandran's plan was wiser than any she had come up with, except the one problem of Kanvar. She doubted Kanvar would agree to his father's assassination. She would have to make Kanvar believe the intent was to free his father from the palace once more rather than kill him. And then, or course, there was the problem of the humans all thinking Kanvar was dead. But Kanvar was the only link she had to be able to call the blue dragons. She did not know their minds, and they were bound to rebuff her thoughts if they felt them at all.

"I think it's a sensible plan," General Zetan said. "Assuming it's not all a lie and a trap."

"Which it undoubtedly is," Qadim said.

"Maybe it is a trap," General Chandran said. "Which is why we should only send the bravest of men who understand exactly what they could be walking into and are willing to take the risk. I am brave enough to go. What about you, Haridas?" Chandran asked the Maran dragon hunter.

Haridas's lips pressed into a thin line, and he fingered his crossbow without answering.

"Someone has to stay here and command our armies as they press upriver," General Zetan said. "What she says about the excessive number of dragons in the area has already been confirmed by my advanced scouts. The full push of this army inland will not be an easy one. If Chandran is going, I have to stay."

Qadim's face twisted into a grim smile. "I want to be the one to put my spear through the Naga king's heart, and I have plenty of men who would risk anything to make that happen. You and your dragon hunters can stay here and fight alongside the soldiers, Haridas, if death and glory doesn't suit you."

Haridas shook his head. "If death and glory are what you want, Qadim, why don't you take your boys after some Great Red volcanic dragon? This is a job for real men, men who use their brains before relying on their brawn. Let me propose this." Haridas walked over to get in Tana's face. "You, pretty little Naga, said you were bound to a Great Green dragon. A matriarch, which means your dragon has children. Young ones, I'd guess from the time of year. What are they, hatchlings?"

Tana's heart raced in a dizzy circle. She opened her mouth, but nothing came out. She couldn't endanger Vasanti and her wyrmlings.

"Answer me!" Haridas shouted in her face. "Or I'll end your life right now, and those cute little dragonlings will be motherless."

"They-they're yearlings," Tana stuttered. "Please, you can't hurt them. They are innocent children."

"Here's the thing then, you hand the wyrmlings over as hostages. If you lead us into a trap, the children will die. If your word is true, they go free. You see, if you have told us the truth, you have nothing to fear and neither do the little ones."

Tana jumped to her feet. "You will not bring the children into this. Would you give your own infant child into the talons of a raptor just to prove you are a man of honor? No, you would not, and neither will I. Kill me now if you like, or follow me, but I will not bow to such a heinous suggestion."

Qadim laughed. "Haridas, you're a fool. Do you really want to come between a Great Green dragon and her wyrmlings? That's more suicidal than facing a Great Red. Stay here if you're too afraid to join General Chandran and me in an assault on the palace. I'll go get my men."

He clapped General Chandran on the back on his way out the door. Haridas shook his head and stalked out behind him.

General Zetan looked down at the maps on the table. "It's risky, Chandran."

"This whole campaign is risky," Chandran said. "I don't see that we have a choice. Just you keep the Nagas focused on your advance so we have a chance to sneak in."

The Varnan general nodded.

"You'll try to contact the Great Blues then?"

"Yes. Come on, Tana is it? Leave your weapons here. Let's go for a walk away from the singing stones."

Tana rose and set the jungle knife on the table, followed by the crossbow and harness. But she returned Parmver's singing stone to its box and tucked it in her belt pouch. "Aren't you worried I'll take control of your mind?"

"You could do that, I suppose," Chandran said. "But if we don't come back here, General Zetan will send half his army after us, with a dozen singing stones. Your control of me and your life would be short."

"Right," Tana said.

Chandran led her out of the colony and down to the beach, then along the sand until they left the soldier encampments far behind, and the song of the stones started to fade. "Is this far enough?" he asked.

Tana tried to use her power to call Kanvar but failed. She shook her head. "There are so many stones."

Chandran took her farther along the shore line, asking every little while if she could use her powers. Finally the sound of the stones faded enough her mind felt close to normal. Tana stopped walking and took a deep breath. The ocean waves rumbled against the shore. The darkness of night clung to the beach.

Neither she nor Chandran had brought a lantern, and the air was thick darkness around them.

"Interesting," Chandran said. "This is much farther than the usual reach of a single singing stone. The effect must be cumulative, the more the stones, the farther they reach."

"Or I'm just more sensitive than other Nagas," Tana said. "You want me to call the blue dragons now?"

"Is Kanvar with them?"

Tana felt as if a leaf-full of rainwater had just been tipped onto her face. "But . . . you said he was dead. You killed him."

Chandran laughed softly. "Well, I did stab him, and I did push him into the ocean. But I know for a fact there was a Great Silver serpent just below the surface. A friend of his. She would not let him die."

Tana could not see Chandran's face in the darkness, but she sensed he was smiling. "I don't understand. Kanvar is a Naga, your enemy. If you knew he would escape death, why did you push him into the water?"

"Tana." Chandran touched her shoulder and then pulled his hand away as if he felt his touch was inappropriate. She was a beautiful young woman, a prisoner, and he an old soldier. In fact, now that she was free of the singing stones, the sense of his presence shocked and confused her. Back at the colony, he had looked and spoken like a hardened, Naga-hating soldier. Now he felt like . . . a friend?

Chandran cleared his throat. "Are you reading my mind?"

Tana's cheeks grew hot. "No, of course not. That would be rude. Parmver was careful to teach me how to keep my mind separate from other people's. I was just . . . feeling your essence."

"My essence?"

Tana couldn't decide if his voice was tinged with sarcasm or mirth. "I was getting a sense of you. Trying to understand what kind of a man you are."

"I'm an old man, Tana. A man who lost both of his sons to the war with the blue dragons. I'm a disappointed and bitter man because the boy I chose to replace them turned out to be a Naga and bonded with the very dragon that killed my boys." Chandran let out a bark of hopeless laughter. "Kanvar. I loved him like a son. And by the fountain, I still do, curse my soul. Why is fate so cruel?"

186

"Is it cruel then that fate has brought you back together again to fight on the same side against true evil?"

"Fate is cruel that such evil should be loosed on this world in the first place and that somehow it survived a thousand years to return in my lifetime. Call him, Tana. Tell him I must speak to him."

Chapter Sixteen

From astride Dharanidhar's back, Kanvar peered through the darkness toward the lights glimmering in the golden palace. *You'd think they'd have gone to sleep by now,* he said to Dharanidhar.

Dharanidhar snorted.

Spurts of blue fire lit up the mountainside across from the golden palace as the Great Blue dragons that were perched around Dharanidhar grew impatient.

They know we're here, Anilon muttered. *They won't let down their guard.*

We should attack them now, one of the younger blue dragons said.

Again? Dhar said. *You've attacked three times already and all you've accomplished is hurting more young gold dragons and getting yourself dazed out of your mind with joy breath. Rajahansa is a coward. He won't come out to fight himself.*

We need to get in there, Anilon mused. *The Nagas must be hiding deep inside the palace. Whether they sleep or not, we attack again while it's still night and we have the advantage. Everyone, ignore the young gold defenders. Drive straight for the palace and get inside. Remember, stay close to me so the singing stone can keep your minds free.*

The blue dragon pride rumbled in agreement.

Dharanidhar chuckled. *Fools, all of you. We are not built for fighting on the ground, let alone in enclosed spaces. What will you do when the young golds come behind and fill the palace with joy breath? You'll have no way out, and Rajahansa will kill every last one of you one-by-one at his leisure, then he'll fly unhindered to Stonefountain. I no longer lead this pride, Anilon, but I'd advise you to rethink your strategy.*

Anilon roared. *So you would have us wait here and do nothing?*

Yes. The human army has already landed. The closer they press to the palace, the more desperate Rajahansa will become. Sooner or later he's going to fly for Stonefountain. Then we take him down while he's out in the open and vulnerable.

Through his link, Kanvar could feel Dharanidhar's claws tighten on the rocky outcrop where he stood, splintering stone as Dhar imagined digging his claws into Rajahansa. The blue dragons of the pride growled in resentment.

Waiting for prey to wander past is for Great Green dragons, the young blue dragon said. *We are blue dragons. We should fight now and keep fighting until Rajahansa is dead.*

Kanvar gritted his teeth. *I don't care what you do, but remember you've all promised to leave my father to me. Strike down Rajahansa, yes, but my father is mine.*

I can't see how that makes any difference, Anilon said.

It makes a difference to me. I want to be with him in his last moments. This evil is not of his doing, and he should not die alone. Kanvar's hand closed around the fist-sized silver decanter he had tucked in a pouch on his belt, the contents of which Bensharie had parted with willingly.

Will you attack now then? Dharanidhar asked Anilon.

Anilon opened his jaws and blue fire crackled between his teeth. *You are right, Dharanidhar,* Anilon said grudgingly. *We are too vulnerable inside the palace. We will have to think of some way to flush Rajahansa out.*

Kanvar grimaced. The air above the canopy was sticky, and clouds covered most of the sky, promising rain. The jungle below them was bare of any creature that could fight in any way since Rajahansa had sent them to fight the humans. But silhouettes of gold dragons lined the palace windows, ready to rebuff any new attack. Kanvar settled in for a good soaking. It didn't seem likely Rajahansa would fly for Stonefountain at night in a rainstorm, but then again that might be exactly when Rajahansa would try for it.

Kanvar? Tana's soft thoughts made contact with his.

Kanvar smiled. He always enjoyed the touch of Tana's mind. *It's the middle of the night, Tana? Why aren't you sleeping?*

Your father asked me to do something for him.

What? Kanvar asked surprised and a little concerned. Perhaps his response had been a bit too sharp because Tana's mind snapped shut to him beyond anything but simple speech. *I'm sorry, Tana. I didn't mean to frighten you. Are you all right?* He tried to make amends.

Kanvar, don't be angry. I'm with someone who wants to talk to you. I just need you to understand, this is what your father wanted.

Kanvar sensed fear from her now, her mind like a startled bird ready to take flight. Something had upset her, and he didn't like the feel of it. *Who are you with, Tana?* he asked gently.

A man named General Chandran. He wants you to come talk to him.

Kanvar stiffened and froze his mind from responding to her until he could think through what she was saying. Tana had gone to Chandran. His father had sent her? But his father would never risk Tana's life by sending her straight into the jaws of the human invaders. She'd be killed. It made no sense, and the realization that Tana was at that moment in enemy hands, a heartbeat away from death, made Kanvar's blood burn like dragon fire.

Kanvar, please, don't block me out. Tana's mind reached out to his like a desperate hand in the darkness. Beyond her shields, he could feel she had a shuddering headache from

191

exposure to singing stones. He could only imagine how many and how close.

I'm still here, Tana. Don't be frightened. I'll come and get you. Has Chandran planned a trap for me? Can you tell?

We are alone on the beach away from the armies and dragon hunters, but we don't have much time before the others come looking for him. I told him about Rajahansa and Khalid. He wants to make an alliance with the blue dragons.

Dharanidhar let a growl vibrate through Kanvar's thoughts into Tana's. *Kanvar and I have no say for the blue dragon pride. Anilon is their leader now.*

Tana gasped, surprised by Dharanidhar's intrusion in their conversation.

"What's wrong, Tana?" Chandran asked. Kanvar could hear a whisper of Chandran's voice through Tana's shields.

"Kanvar says . . . well, his dragon says." Tana broke off speaking, her mind tumbling into confusion, oppressed by exhaustion and pain from exposure to the singing stones.

Relax, Tana. It's all right. I'm coming. I'll bring the leader of the blue dragon pride with me. If Chandran wants to negotiate a partnership, he can do it. Kanvar sent her a feeling of reassurance and then left her mind alone, just keeping enough contact that he could feel her presence and find his way to her.

"His dragon says what?" Chandran asked Tana.

Tana took a deep breath and tried to steady her mind. She'd gotten dizzy while trying to carry on more than one conversation at once and keep the thought from Kanvar that she intended to kill his father. No way would he help her if he knew. Now, her head throbbed, but she'd done what was necessary. He would come talk to Chandran.

"Tana?" Chandran prodded.

"Sorry." Tana rubbed her head. "I just can't talk to two people at once, let alone more." Dharanidhar's presence in her mind had been a surprise. If she'd thought about it, she'd have expected him, but she hadn't.

·"Are you all right?" Chandran once again touched her shoulder but left his hand there this time as a show of concern.

"As fine as you'd expect with all those singing stones back there."

"And Kanvar's answer?"

"He said he'd come talk to you, but his dragon is no longer in command of the blue dragon pride. He said he'd bring their leader along with him to negotiate with you."

Chandran shifted and unslung his crossbow. "How long until they get here?" he asked while he loaded it.

"Having a loaded weapon in hand isn't the best way to gain allies," Tana said.

"Showing weakness isn't a good way to gain allies either."

"I don't know how long they'll be." Tana wished she had her own weapons. She trusted Kanvar and his dragon, but not any others.

While they waited, it started to rain. Tana relished the patter of the rain on her armor. Unlike when she wore her clothes from the village, she did not feel wet inside the armor. The water just rolled off of her. She could lift her dragonhide hood over her head to keep her hair dry but chose not to. The sound of the rain on the beach mixed with the crash and hiss of the waves.

Time passed in silence until Chandran spoke again.

"Perhaps we should have brought a lantern so they could find us in the dark."

"My mind is a lantern linked to Kanvar's. He can feel me and sense where to come."

The flap of great wings sounded above the water. Chandran pivoted to face the ocean and readied his crossbow. "They snuck up behind us."

"You didn't think we'd fly over all your soldiers and their ballistae did you?" Kanvar's voice called out through the darkness as two giant dragon shapes settled into the sand.

"Did you bring the singing stone?" Chandran asked as Kanvar's dragon lowered him to the ground and Kanvar limped up to him.

"No. It is in use with the blue dragons who are watching the palace to be sure Rajahansa does not escape. Besides, how will you negotiate with Anilon if I can't hear what he says to tell you?"

"I suppose you have a point." Chandran tightened his grip on the crossbow.

"Kanvar." Tana reached out to him, and Kanvar took her hand and kissed it.

"Tana. I thought you were watching Vasanti's wyrmlings while she hunted."

"She finished hunting." Tana could feel Kanvar's concern for her. He didn't think she should have left the safety of Vasanti's lair. He felt he was already doing what was necessary to stop Rajahansa from sacrificing his father to raise Khalid from the fountain.

Tana pulled her hand back from him. "You think you can do everything yourself, but you're wrong. And just like when we went hunting together, you still won't believe that I can be anything more than a helpless village woman."

"Tana, that's not how it is."

"That's exactly how it is. I'm a full Naga now. Don't think you can hide your thoughts from me."

Kanvar's mind closed up tightly from her. "I worry just as much about Devaj, so don't take it personally."

"Stop it," Chandran said. "I don't have time for bickering. Tana tells me we must kill your father. She believes you won't do it. I have an alternate solution."

"Hold on." Kanvar's voice turned icy. "She came to you for help to kill my father?"

"Kanvar, please. You have to understand." Tana's heart pattered like the falling rain. Chandran had been blunt instead of delicate. She feared Kanvar's reaction.

"Oh, I understand. But I didn't think *you* did." Kanvar fingered the hilt of his father's sword.

"You really do think I'm an ignorant girl, don't you?" Tana's hands balled into fists.

"No, Tana. But this is a delicate matter. It's my father's life we're talking about here. He's an innocent man."

"Your father is innocent, yes, but his dragon is a murderer and worse. He has to be stopped, and this beach is lined with people who have come to do just that. All they need is to know where the palace is and have a way to get in."

Kanvar's armor rasped as he shifted to confront Chandran. "It's delightful to see you again." His tone was ironic, almost mocking.

"Too bad we can't actually see each other in the dark," Chandran said. The tone of his voice was mocking as well, but Tana could feel an undercurrent of fondness from him.

"And it's just as wet now as it was last time," Kanvar said.

"It was wet for you then, not me. I'm not that fond of swimming. But tell me, Kanvar, . . . where's Kumar Raza. Last we spoke, you implied that you left him on the island with the dead red dragon. He wasn't there. In fact, he doesn't seem to be anywhere. You told me you didn't kill him or hurt his mind."

Kanvar let out a little laugh. "Kumar Raza? I suppose Tana told you he's my grandfather?"

"I got that idea from her, yes. It must be uncomfortable being a Naga and having the Great Dragon Hunter as your grandfather."

Tana bit her lip. She felt squeezed by the confrontation between these two men. The blue dragons shifted in the sand. One of them opened its jaws, showing the blue fire stoked in its throat.

Kanvar laughed again. "He wants me dead every bit as badly as you do, and I hold you responsible for making sure the Varnan dragon hunters know that."

Tana felt Chandran's hands tighten on the stalk of his crossbow. His mind tumbled with conflicting thoughts and emotion. Kanvar was an enemy; he must be killed. Kanvar was a son; he should be protected. Kumar Raza was Kanvar's grandfather. Raza was required to kill Kanvar. Raza loved his grandson, and the two must have gone together to fight the red dragon. To protect Kumar Raza, the Varnan dragon hunters must never know this.

Tana had to concentrate to block his streaming thoughts from her own mind. Parmver had not exaggerated how hard it could be at times, especially when her head already hurt from the singing stones.

"All right," Chandran said. "But where is he?"

"Last time he visited Stonefountain, he found a scroll that had a map of the world. An ancient map that showed the world was round. And he is, well, Kumar Raza, and the thought that he might return to Kundiland by sailing eastward was more than he could pass up. There is another continent over there." Kanvar fell silent, his mind too blocked for Tana to tell what he was thinking.

"You came to Kundiland from the east?" Chandran said.

"Yes, but flying is faster than sailing. I left him shortly after you killed me. Haven't seen him since, but Chandran, you should know . . . as I passed over the continent, I saw signs of a Naga civilization that remained after Stonefountain fell. Cut off from this side of the world. I believe there are other Nagas there. I don't know how many."

"More Nagas?" Chandran let out a stream of expletives that seemed a bit impolite for a gray-haired old man, but perhaps fitting for a soldier.

"I'm sorry." Kanvar's voice was soft.

"Are you done catching up with each other?" Tana said. "Because that Varnan general and the dragon hunters did not seem like they would wait all night. Kanvar, ask the blue dragon leader if he and his dragons would be willing to fly General Chandran and a team of dragon hunters up to the palace and keep the gold dragons busy, so the dragon hunters can do what needs to be done." Tana hated to interrupt but felt that Kanvar was avoiding talk of killing Rajahansa.

A thunderous roar from one of the blue dragons shook the night. Blue fire split the darkness.

"Brilliant," Tana said. "We're trying to be secret here, and he goes and wakes the whole army."

Cries from the startled soldiers rang from the army encampments.

"Was that a yes or a no?" General Chandran asked Kanvar.

"That was an emphatic yes from Anilon, the leader of the pride, unless your soldiers decide to attack him right now. The blue dragons will do whatever it takes to stop Khalid's return."

"My Varnan counterpart will keep the armies in check. He knows I've come out here to talk to you. Well, not to you, to the blue dragon with Tana translating. Officially, you are dead, Kanvar, and you must stay that way. That means that you can't be present when we attack the palace," Chandran said.

"I will not agree to that," Kanvar said. "I already have an arrangement with the blue dragons that I get to be with my father when they kill Rajahansa. I will not let him die alone. It is too cruel. I will have the same agreement from you, or we don't work together. You and your men must not touch my father. You kill his dragon. I get to spend his last few moments with him."

The leader of the blue dragon pride roared again, snatched Kanvar up in his foreclaw, and shook him. Tana could see the dragon's actions in the blue glow of its dragonstone and the fire that crackled between its teeth.

"What's the dragon saying?" Chandran whispered to Tana.

"I'm sorry, I wasn't listening. This is all new to me." Tana opened her mind to speech with the blue dragon leader, but Anilon, dropped Kanvar in the sand without further comment.

Kanvar groaned and dragged himself to his feet. "Anilon says that he will not allow my sentiments to get in the way of destroying Rajahansa. He cares nothing for my father. He accepts your idea and will return tomorrow with as many dragons as you need to carry your men. But you must swear to keep your soldiers from attacking his pride."

"Agreed. I'll bring Qadim and his best dragon hunters."

Tana barely heard Chandran's acceptance of the terms as Kanvar's emotions overflowed and pressed past her shields. He was heartsick and desperate to get to his father. There had to be some way.

"I'll go," Tana said. "I can be with him in your place. I'll tell him how much you love him and don't want him to suffer."

"You?" Hope blossomed in Kanvar's heart.

"Yes."

"In the middle of a battle like that? You could be killed."

"A lot of people and dragons will die tomorrow. I may or may not be one of them, but I won't sit back and do nothing. I am as fond of King Amar as you are. You're right. If he has to die, someone should be with him. I will go in your place whether you like it or not. It's not your decision. It's mine."

"Tana." The fingers of Kanvar's crippled hand reached through the darkness to caress her face along with the rain that continued to sprinkle. His hand shook. His voice shook. "I love you."

Before Tana could answer, he clasped her hand with his good hand, pulled her to him, and pressed his cool rain-soaked lips against hers. Tana's face grew hot, and her heart swelled in her chest, expanding outward, sending tingles through her extremities. She kissed him back, desperate to hold on to that moment. They had shared too few moments together. Always they seemed cut short with goodbyes. He was fire and passion to her, life as full as all the jungle as their lips moved against each other.

His mind opened up to her, showing a memory of what had happened when he went to Maran to stop the Naga there: how it was Kumar Raza's brother Rajan, how they had killed the red dragon that held him captive, but saved Rajan from death by helping him bond with a new dragon at the moment of the death of his old.

Tana gasped and realized that Kanvar had pressed a small decanter into her hand as he held it. The hot metal bit into her palm as her hand tightened on it.

Bensharie's blood. Kanvar ran his fingers through her hair. *I'm counting on you to save my father. Please . . . please help him survive this. Defend him against the dragon hunters. They will turn on you and him the moment the others are dead. You understand that?* He kissed her again, leaving her breathless.

Tears streamed down Kanvar's face.

Tana reached up and wiped the tears away, but the rain continued to wet his cheeks. *Vasanti will get us both out alive. Tell the blue dragons not to harm her when she comes for me.*

I will. I love you.

"I love you too," Tana said aloud. Reluctantly she stepped back away from Kanvar.

Dharanidhar lifted Kanvar up onto his neck, and the two blue dragons flew away. Chandran chuckled softly as he and Tana walked back toward the Maran colony. "You and Kanvar, what a surprise."

"You don't think Nagas can fall in love?" Tana slipped the decanter into one of her belt pouches, hoping Chandran wouldn't notice in the darkness.

"If they didn't, the world wouldn't have to worry about more Naga children being born, would it?" His voice held a cold edge to it, and she felt his fear of the Nagas and revulsion for what they could do to a person's mind. It was not just his duty as a soldier that led him to hunt them. He genuinely wanted them gone from the face of the world. Except Kanvar. He hated himself for his weakness in loving Kanvar, but he couldn't help it.

Tana blinked and put her shields back up. She was tired and having a hard time staying out of Chandran's mind. "You know, General," she said. "Kanvar believes that as long as the humans have the dragonstones there may be some way for humans and Nagas to live peacefully together. The other Nagas hate him for that. They believe the humans want only to murder them all. But you and Kanvar are proof that there can be some compromise, some interchange, between humans and Nagas. What do you think?"

"Surely you already know. My mind has been exposed to you for some time now."

"My head hurts too much and I'm so tired, I'm having a hard enough time just trying to keep your mind from plowing over mine like a rampaging camdor. I'm glad we're into range of the singing stones, at least they will give me some protection from your overwhelming sense of purpose. You obviously hate Nagas and want to kill us all, I get that. But . . . if things were different, if you could be sure the Nagas posed no threat to the freedom of humanity, would you consider living beside them in peace?"

Chandran stopped at the head of the beach within calling distance of the Maran Colony walls, and well into the range of the singing stones. "You're accusing me of hurting your mind? Me, a human, hurting a Naga? Are you implying that I have as much impact on a Naga's mind as the Naga might have on mine? Is that possible?"

Tana pressed the heel of her hands to her forehead. "The power, it's hard to control, and I'm new to it. The thoughts of every creature in the jungle tend to press into my mind, and I sometimes have a hard time maintaining my own identity. You are a strong-willed man, General. Some of your thoughts are like ballista fire into my own. It takes a good deal of effort to block them."

"So, a human can impact the Naga mind. If that's so, then perhaps there is a way for a human to block a Naga mind as well." Chandran fingered his crossbow and stared off into the dark sky in the direction Kanvar had flown.

"If there was, then would you say there is hope of co-existence between Nagas and humans?" Tana wanted to believe Kanvar was right, and that when this war was over there could be hope for the two of them to settle down together in peace without being hunted by the humans.

"Perhaps," Chandran said. "But there is nothing in history to suggest that would be the case. I've studied everything I could get my hands on, and there is no reference to humans having any chance against Naga power without the singing stones."

"Well." Tana took a deep breath. Since Kanvar had already mentioned Kumar Raza to Chandran, perhaps it was alright to talk about him. "Parmver said Kumar Raza has learned how to shield his mind from the Nagas. Perhaps other humans could learn to do it as well."

"Perhaps." Chandran took hold of Tana's arm in a strong grip. "What did Kanvar give you when you kissed?"

Tana sucked in a surprised breath at his sudden attack on her person and change of topic. "What? I . . ."

"He handed you something. You put it in your belt, what was it? The night might be dark, but I'm not stupid." He gave her a little shake.

"It . . . it was, is . . . medicine, so his father won't feel anything when Rajahansa is killed. Kanvar doesn't want his father to suffer." A lie, but she didn't dare tell Chandran the truth. The general would never let her go to the palace with him if he thought she had any plan for saving a descendant of Khalid.

"I warn you, Tana. If you, Kanvar, or the blue dragons betray me, you will pay dearly."

Tana tore away from him. "It is I, General, who should worry about betrayal. I know you intend to kill me the moment you've finished with the others." Tana let out a bitter laugh. "Even after I help you stop the biggest Naga threat to this world since the fall of Stonefountain, you will slay me. You feel you have no choice. So don't talk to me about betrayal. I've known my life was forfeit from the moment I decided to come to you. So be it. Tomorrow will be the great day of slaughter. I wonder if any human, Naga, or dragon will be alive at the end of it."

Long before full dawn bathed the sky with sunshine, Devaj left the new village and wondered out onto the beach. The waves lapped the sand, hissing in and out. He couldn't say why he'd gotten up so early. A stiff breeze blew sand against his face and arms and kept the morning mist away. The stars above were fading. He rubbed his head. It hurt for some reason. He'd slept, but the exhaustion had not left him. It felt like some dark wave had washed over him and was dragging him down below the water and out to sea.

Tearing his mind back from the darkness, he licked his salt-kissed lips and glanced out across the horizon. A flock of sea birds like black silhouettes flew toward him. So many, and they grew bigger as they approached.

Devaj startled backwards as he realized they were dragons not birds, so many they covered the sky. He could not see their color in the darkness, but as they approached he saw every dragon carried a rider. Their minds washed over him. They were gold dragons and each had a Naga. The immensity of it tore his breath from him. He stood frozen, unable to breathe, unable to move. These were Nagas. An army of Nagas. It could not be real. Must be a dream. He was sleeping and only thought he had awakened.

A gold dragon, almost as big as Rajahansa, spiraled down to the beach. A man slid from his neck and strode over to Devaj. "My name is Lord Theodoric. I have come to serve my king."

Devaj opened his mouth to speak but could not think what to say. The dark wave returned and dragged his mind into unconsciousness.

About The Author

Rebecca Shelley (Rebecca Lyn Shelley) is the author of over 30 published books including the bestselling **Smart-boys Club** series as well as the popular **Red Dragon Codex** and **Brass Dragon Codex**. She loves writing about dragons and is excited to be writing the **Dragonbound** series. Her **Aos Si** *trilogy* will thrill fans of YA Paranormal Romance. To learn more or contact her, visit her website http://www.rebeccashelley.com.

If you have enjoyed reading **Dragonbound VI: Green Dragon**, Rebecca would love to have you post a review on the site where you purchased it.

Coming Soon:

Dragonbound VII: Gold Dragon Preview
By Rebecca Shelley

Prologue

I have spent my life living peacefully, caring for the dragons and other creatures around me, wanting for nothing, and needing nothing more than I have: a home, a beautiful wife, two incredible sons, and a dragon companion who has through the last five hundred years been a second heartbeat to mine, a mind to match my own, a friend, and a councilor. I never could have dreamed that my life could change so quickly from happiness to torment. Surely this is just a nightmare from which I will wake and see a golden sunrise over the steamy jungle.

Amar

Chapter One

Amar stood with his hands on the smooth golden windowsill and watched the rising sun chase the fog off the treetops below. Behind him Rajahansa snorted in his sleep and shifted. He'd wake soon, and Amar's moments of mental freedom would end. He thought about casting himself out the window, but the young gold dragons on either side of him would grab him once again the moment he put his first foot up on the windowsill. Rajahansa wasn't taking any chances with his life.

The arms of the mountains reached out in a bowl shape, surrounding the jungle valley below. As daylight lit the sky, the circle of blue dragons perched along the mountain cliffs became visible. They'd been there at sunset, and they were still there now. Rajahansa would be furious when he woke. Thank the fountain, Kanvar had gotten

Amar's message from Tana. Amar was confident the blue dragons would never let Rajahansa leave the palace again.

On the jungle floor, the Black River wound its way through the trees, flowing down the mountains and out past the jungle village to the ocean beyond. Rajahansa's scouts had confirmed the arrival of the human armies.

Did you think you could hide from them forever? Khalid's voice like sludge swept through Amar's mind. *Grandson, really, there is only one solution to the human problem.*

Amar blocked Khalid's destructive thoughts that came to his mind from the waking Rajahansa's. If only Rajahansa had not let himself be seduced by the tyrant, things would be different. Yes, the humans would still come, but the world was a big place and dragons could fly to places human armies would never reach.

You would run and hide like a dung beetle? Rajahansa mocked him.

"This conflict is pointless. The world is big enough for all of us." Amar turned from the window to face his dragon. Rajahansa lay curled in the center of the chamber. His golden plates shone in the pale morning light from the window. He had scars now that he'd never had before, scars Kanvar's dragon had given him on the day Kanvar had bonded, and others Anilon had inflicted. Rajahansa had not forgotten that, nor forgiven it. Amar had been foolish to think that he would.

The smell of breakfast cooking in the palace kitchens lingered on the air. Bellori, the young gold dragon in charge of serving food to the king, would bring it soon: roasted bovinder for Rajahansa, fruit and honeyed milk for Amar. Just like every other morning . . . and not.

You are right, Amar. Today will be a day remembered in the history of the world forever as the day you and I rose to greatness and power. Rajahansa stood, spread his wings, and shook away the sleep.

"If you try for Stonefountain, today will be the day the blue dragons kill us. Have no doubt, Rajahansa. They will not let Khalid return to this world."

Khalid's dark laughter pulsed through Amar's shields. Khalid said something to Rajahansa, but Amar refused to hear it. He would not listen to Khalid's lies and promises.

You're a fool, Rajahansa told Amar. *Stonefountain has had a thousand years to regain its power, a thousand years worth of souls added to replace those that were torn from it. You cannot deny this truth. It is evident in the seed of your blood. Five hundred years you tried to have Naga children and failed. It is Stonefountain that imbues the Nagas with power. Wounded, it could bring precious few Nagas to life. Now look, in one generation: Karishi, Rajan, Devaj, Kanvar, Tana, Aadi, and Denali. Our numbers have more than doubled. It is the fountain itself that calls us to it. It's time that true civilization is restored.*

"I hear Khalid's voice in your words. The old civilization was corrupt and evil. It should be purged from memory, not restored."

Rajahansa bared his teeth and roared at Amar. *Do not anger me or I'll let Khalid take your mind again. I know how much you enjoy his company.*

Amar shuddered. Khalid and Rajahansa together could so easily tear through his shields, and when they did, Khalid was never gentle. Amar's stomach twisted and the smell of food sickened him suddenly. He was a prisoner here in the palace where he'd always been safe before—his mind bound and tormented by his enemies beyond any physical punishment a human jailor could contrive. He turned back to the window, hands shaking. "Rajahansa, I beg you one more time. Rid your mind of this connection to Khalid. Before you do anything more, sever the link and think freely again for a while."

Rajahansa grabbed him and flung him across the room so he hit the floor and slid up against the wall. *Silence. You sicken me.*

"The feeling is mutual."

Rajahansa gave him a mental slap and would have turned Khalid loose on him again, but a pair of gold dragons swooped in through the window and landed.

Your Majesty, the older of the two dragons said, bowing. *The human armies are moving up the river toward the village, half in boats and half on land. They have engaged with the dragon army.*

So be it, Rajahansa said. *The humans think they can win, but they will fail.*

We spotted a flight of blue dragons out by the coast, the scout said.

Good. If the humans and blues fight each other, all the better for us. Gather all the gold dragons and be ready to fight. The blues will not hold us here. Our destiny awaits elsewhere. Rajahansa shooed the scouts away and called for Bellori to bring breakfast.

Amar remained where he'd been thrown. If there was anything he could do to fight Rajahansa, surely he would do it but the power was beyond him now. His best hope was to remain quiet and unnoticed so Rajahansa and Khalid would leave him alone.

Majesty, Bellori's gentle thoughts stirred him sometime later. *Your breakfast.* Bellori put a tray of sweet bread, fruit, and honeyed milk on the ground beside him and eased him up to sit with his back against the wall.

"I'm not hungry." He pushed away the cup of milk Bellori held out to him and noticed that Rajahansa had already eaten and left the chamber. Amar's two dragon guards still flanked the window.

You must be; you didn't eat last night. Bellori said.

Bellori, Amar rubbed the young dragon's neck while whispering into his mind. *I don't want you to fight today. Leave the palace now. Rajahansa expects you to fly back and forth between here and the herds you keep. He won't question you leaving the palace. You're small enough to get down below the canopy. Go down, and stay down, no matter what happens up here. Promise me you will.*

Bellori quivered. *Rajahansa will kill me.*

No. He and I are leaving today. He won't even notice. Go back to the kitchens now then get away while no one is looking. Amar patted Bellori and urged him to go.

I will on one condition, Bellori said. *You eat your breakfast.*

Amar chuckled and took the cup of milk. "If you insist."

I do. Bellori bowed, glanced nervously over his shoulder at the two dragon guards at the window, then slid out of the room.

Amar took a sip of the honey-sweetened milk, but the sudden roar of the dragon guards tumbled the cup from his hand. Not just the two guards in this chamber, but dragons at each of the windows let out a roar of alarm. Amar jumped to his feet and watched as what had to be every adult dragon of the blue dragon pride closed in on the palace. The gold dragon defenders took to the air to stop them.

Rajahansa stormed into the chamber. *On my neck, now!* he ordered Amar.

Amar took a deep breath. *Please, Kanvar,* he thought as he climbed onto Rajahansa's lowered neck. *Don't let me down.*

Kanvar will not stop us, Rajahansa spit into his mind. *Don't even try to contact him. You know I'll just block you.*

Amar flinched as Rajahansa lifted his head, locking the plate over Amar to hold him in place. Rajahansa climbed up onto the window sill and lifted his wings, ready to launch into the air the moment the gold dragons managed to punch a hole in the circle of attacking blues. Amar blinked. Something was wrong. The blues were not in a retaining circle but were driving straight for the palace in a wedge-shaped formation. The new tactic took the gold dragons off guard, scattering them like butterflies in the wind.

Seeing his chance to break free, Rajahansa roared and took to the air. He need only fly to one side or other of the wedge and he'd be gone. Haidar and Liander astride their dragons came up on either side of him as the full force of the blue dragons headed toward them.

The gold dragons reformed and descended on the wedge, filling the air with their joy breath, but the blue dragons ignored them. They breathed no fire and made no move against the golds. They're holding their breath, Amar realized, so the joy breath won't affect them.

Rajahansa dove low and made a break for the coast followed by Haidar and Liander. Blue fire shot up from beneath him, burning his belly. Amar looked down and saw five of the largest and fiercest blue dragons launch up from the top of the canopy where they had been waiting. Amar's heart beat to match the flap of wings as the blue dragons closed the narrow gap. I'm going to die, he realized.

He'd been waiting for this, but the shock of it stole his breath, and all at once he didn't want to die, though he knew he had to. He expected the blue dragons to hit the golds' underbellies with claw and teeth as they were want to fight, but the blues came up level with the golds instead.

Dragonbound VI

The sudden shriek of singing stones sliced through Amar's mind. The pain was so surprising and intense, he could hardly see to realize that the blue dragon, which had risen up beside him, was carrying dragon hunters in his claws.

Other Books by Rebecca Shelley

Aos Si Trilogy

Middle Grade Fantasy

YA Fantasy

Epic Fantasy Romance

Epic Fantasy